LEFT TO RIGHT

This book won first prize in the Scripture Union
competition for new writers.

LEFT TO RIGHT

Eileen Taylor

SCRIPTURE UNION
130 City Road, London EC1V 2NJ

©Eileen Taylor 1985

First published 1985

ISBN 0 86201 295 3

Phototypeset by Wyvern Typesetting Limited, Bristol
Printed and bound in Great Britain by
Cox and Wyman Ltd, Reading

1

As Paul became aware of sunlight beyond his bedroom curtains, he stretched and turned over beneath the quilt, waiting sleepily for the chuckles from the next room which would tell him that Katy was also awake. Almost two years old, Katy was a small bundle of fun and, though he would never admit it to his friends at school, Paul thought the world of her. Anything he did to amuse her was a huge success and produced a toothy grin and giggles. At first, when Katy was a tiny baby, Paul hadn't been impressed with her and wondered what all the fuss was about. Gradually, he began to see possibilities, and, while he still grumbled about having to keep all his things out of her reach, he decided she was worth having around.

Just as he was dropping into a doze, he heard the jingle of a rattle, followed by the soft thud of a teddy being unceremoniously dumped out of the cot. Paul padded through in bare feet and reached into the cot. Two chubby arms clasped his pyjama jacket and a soggy kiss landed somewhere on his shoulder. He hugged Katy as he carried her to his own room and deposited her on the floor with some ancient books and plastic beakers. She, on the other hand, seemed more interested in his slippers and pulled out the soles. That completed, she sucked a sock while looking round for other excitement. Paul found that he could keep her happy by supplying her with oddments from his cupboards. That way she would not disturb Dad and Mum.

Katy seemed intent on emptying the bottom drawer of his cupboard, and Paul watched her absently, thinking of school, but something was niggling at the back of his mind. Something that had been puzzling him for a while was now becoming downright worrying, especially after last night. Some time after going to bed he had heard Dad and Mum begin to argue again. Quietly at first, it soon grew louder and angrier. Mum was saying that Dad didn't understand – at least that's what it sounded like. Dad shouted that he didn't and then the door had slammed as Dad had gone out. Paul had sat up in bed, hugging his knees, listening to Mum crying downstairs for what had seemed a very long time. When all was quiet he had drifted off to sleep, but it had been really frightening and he shivered at the memory.

To comfort himself, he picked up Katy and played 'This little piggy went to market' with her toes. She squeaked ''gain, 'gain,' over and over, until all her fingers and toes had been tweaked three or four times and Paul had forgotten his worries.

Mum came in to dress Katy and take her down for breakfast.

'Anything special at school today, Paul?' asked Mum, when Paul appeared in the kitchen.

'No, not today, but Sports Afternoon is next month, Mum. I can't wait – I'm going to win every race this year, for sure.'

'For sure?' queried Mum, handing Paul his cereal.

'Yes, for sure. I've really practised and anyway, running is about the only thing I'm good at and I'm going to show them all.'

'Well, you certainly do have practice. The time you leave here for school I'm surprised you're not late every day. Rebecca Allen passes the house ten minutes before you leave.'

'Huh!' grunted Paul, 'Rebecca Allen!' He didn't feel he needed to say anything else, after putting so much scorn into the name of his Public Enemy Number One.

6

Rebecca Allen was a pest. Whatever she did, she was good at – Maths, English, Art, Recorder – with one exception. It gave Paul great satisfaction that when it came to running, Rebecca Allen seemed to have two left feet. In short, she was useless at sports.

'School, Paul!' shouted Mum, interrupting his thoughts. 'Quick! Shoes, bag, dinner money, anorak – now run!' She blew him a kiss as he ran out of the house, bag and coat flying behind him. He was sure he was good enough to win all the races and felt a thrill of excitement at the thought. He ran across the park, past the shops and up the hill towards school. Here he was slowed down by groups of children straggling across the pavement, but still he arrived at the gate just as the bell shrilled out.

In a few moments Paul sank down at his desk, out of breath but all the more confident of his ability. Yes, he could see it now. Paul Walker, European Champion, Olympic Champion, Champion of the World! Then he paused in his dream. How could the running champion of the world be called Walker? That would have to go!

'Paul Walker! Paul Walker!' Miss Shaw was repeating his name and looking none too pleased.

'Er, yes, Miss Shaw?' Paul sat up and tried to look interested.

'Paul, please listen, or you will not know what to do for the rest of the morning.'

'Yes, Miss Shaw,' and he struggled to follow the apparently endless list of things his group had to get through before lunchtime.

Break time came as a welcome relief and he hung around outside the cloakroom for his own gang of friends. There were about five of them, all boys of course, who enjoyed a real rough and tumble in the playground, or on the field if it was dry. When the sound of the bell put an end to their fun, they shuffled unwillingly back into class.

After lunch there was P.E. and today Miss Shaw had promised to have a sports practice if the weather was fine. As they all trooped on to the playing field, Paul's face lit up at the prospect of doing something well at last. He quite liked Miss Shaw and rather looked forward to her approval. Miss Shaw divided them into three groups of boys and three groups of girls. Then each group ran the length of the field, starting together.

'Well done, Paul!' shouted Miss Shaw, as he ran across the finishing line a few feet ahead of the next boy. 'Well done!' she repeated, looking slightly surprised. Paul felt a glow inside and he even ventured a grin. Then Miss Shaw turned her attention to the next group of boys at the starting line. While he watched, Paul kept on the move, jogging up and down until it was the turn of the last group of girls. There she was! R.A. herself – with a worried look on her face! When the rest of the group had crossed the finishing line, Rebecca Allen was only half-way there, her legs looking as if they weren't quite sure what they were doing.

'Never mind, Rebecca!' called Miss Shaw. 'Good try!'

'Good try!' thought Paul. 'Absolutely pathetic, if you ask me!'

'Not a bad day, today,' he thought as he wandered home from school – making sure, of course, that Rebecca left well ahead of him. 'Not a bad day at all! Wait till I tell Mum about the practice!' And at the thought of how pleased she would be, he started to jog, not stopping until he turned in at the gate of his house. He tried the back door, but it was locked. That was a surprise as Mum was usually in when he got home from school, but he knew where the spare key was hidden and soon opened the door. Everything was very tidy in the kitchen.

'Mum must have gone out with Katy to do some shopping,' he thought, so he poured some milk and helped himself to a biscuit. After a few minutes he decided to run down to the shops to meet them and set off at a cracking pace. But despite peering through shop windows, he couldn't catch a glimpse of them. He ran back home and flopped in front of the television. Of all the days for Mum to be out when he had such good news to tell her!

He was so engrossed in watching the cartoons that he didn't hear Dad come in until he stood in front of the screen.

'Where's your Mum?' he asked. 'There's no tea ready.'

'I don't know,' said Paul. 'But Dad, I came first in the sports practice at school, and Miss Shaw . . .'

'I've no time to listen now,' interrupted Dad. 'I'm going up to get changed.' With that, Dad left the room. Paul shrugged and turned back to the television.

Suddenly, the door of the lounge flew open and Dad stood there, staring at a piece of paper he was clutching in his hand. The look on his face made Paul shiver.

'She's gone!' Dad shouted, banging the door post with his fist.

'Who's gone?' whispered Paul, hardly daring to ask.

'Your Mum, that's who! She's gone and taken Katy with her. She says,' and he glared at the letter again, 'she says she can't take any more, so she's going away.' He threw the letter on to a chair.

'Mum gone?' repeated Paul, as if he couldn't believe his ears. 'Mum and Katy gone? No – no . . .'

'Come back here, Paul!' yelled Dad, but it was too late. Paul was out of the door and running – running he didn't know where. Anywhere away from that dreadful letter, from the fact that Mum had gone!

2

It was much later that evening that Paul wearily dragged his feet up the path to the kitchen door. He hardly remembered where he had been, only that he had tried to get as far away as he could. After running for what had felt like miles, he had crumpled on the edge of a pavement. He had then realised he had nowhere to go, no money and no food. If he went to a friend's house they would just take him home. If he stayed on the streets he would be cold and hungry. There was nothing for it but to go back to the house and Dad – and he would probably be furious and shout at him.

Paul opened the kitchen door very quietly, hoping to creep in unnoticed. Dad was hunched on a chair at the kitchen table, his head in his hands, Mum's letter on the floor. It looked as if he had been sitting like that for a very long time. He jerked his head up when he heard Paul's step.

'You're back, then!' he said, almost as if it didn't matter.

'Yes.'

'Silly thing to do, running off like that! As if I don't have enough on my mind!' Yet Dad wasn't ranting and raving.

'Can I get a drink?' enquired Paul, cautiously.

'What? Oh yes, yes – and pour one out for me, too. I haven't had anything since I came home from work.'

Paul handed Dad a glass of lemonade and put the biscuit tin in the middle of the table. Then he sat opposite Dad with his own drink. Suddenly, Dad straightened up and looked at Paul.

'Look, son!' he said, 'You're old enough now to do your share around here, now that . . .' He paused and glanced down at the letter before continuing, 'now that your mum's gone.' Paul winced at the words. It was true! She had gone. And Dad didn't seem to care.

'So, I've been thinking,' went on Dad. 'I'll see you off to school and lock the house in the mornings before work, and you'll have to let yourself in at tea-time and wait for me.'

'What about in the holidays?' thought Paul. 'What about my tea?' But he kept quiet.

'Now between us,' Dad was warming to the subject now, 'we'll sort out the washing and suchlike. There's nothing to it really.'

Paul could contain himself no longer. 'Where's she gone? My mum?' he asked, not looking at Dad.

'That's none of your business,' replied Dad, staring blankly at the letter again. 'None of your business.'

'But is she coming back, Dad?'

Dad raised his head and looked Paul straight in the eye.

'That's up to her, son, but if she thinks I'm going begging her to come back, she's got another think coming. I'll show her we can do without her. Now, get off to bed and no nonsense!'

Despite feeling very hungry, Paul scrambled upstairs and into bed as quickly as he could. Dad had his spirit back and Paul didn't want a smack to add to his troubles.

Next morning he woke early and strained his ears for the sound of Katy in the next room. Suddenly, like a weight dropping on him, he remembered. Katy wasn't there – might never be there again. How could Mum do that? She must have loved Katy more than him to have taken Katy away with her. Then a horrible thought came to him. Mum couldn't have loved him at all or she wouldn't have left him! At that, a great sob broke out of him; then he shook himself and clenched his teeth. All

11

right, if she didn't love him, he didn't love her any more. He viciously threw off the quilt and began to dress. All his clothes were in a heap just where he had dropped them the night before and as no one had sorted out which were clean and which were dirty, he emerged from his bedroom looking somewhat dishevelled.

The house was quiet. Dad was still asleep, so Paul tiptoed down to the kitchen for something to eat. At least he knew what to do now. He would stick with Dad and never even think of Mum and Katy. They had left him and he would show them he could manage without them, just like Dad. His inside was all knotted up, but he managed to gulp down some cereal and bread. It was still early – too early to be bored already. He fiddled around aimlessly with the cereal packet and began to think of school. He had almost forgotten the thrill of yesterday's success. Now would be a good time to practise when the streets were empty, so a few minutes later he was off, jogging round the block, across the park and back by the shops. How strange it was to be out and about with the postmen and milkmen, but there were others with the same idea. He felt embarrassed when other people caught sight of him, but the older joggers in their coloured tracksuits simply grinned and jogged on. By the time he was home, he barely had time to tell Dad where he had been before it was time to leave for school.

Perhaps if he kept busy he would forget everything else. If Miss Shaw was surprised to see Paul Walker with his head down over his work all morning, she didn't show it. Nor did she appear to notice that his hair was unbrushed and his shirt fastened on the wrong button, but at lunch-time she dropped into Mrs Mitchell's office.

'Have you heard whether there is anything wrong at Paul Walker's house?' she asked the headmistress.

'No one has been in touch with me,' said Mrs Mitchell, 'and I'm sure they'd have let us know if there was anything serious. Why? Is there anything wrong with Paul?'

'Not exactly. I just have a feeling that something might be different. Never mind – it's probably my imagination.'

However, a few minutes later, Paul appeared at the door of the staff room and it took no imagination at all to see what had happened. His nose was bleeding and there were one or two bruises appearing on his legs.

'Wait till you see Sandy Graham!' said the dinner lady, her arm resting firmly on Paul's shoulder. 'I don't know what got into them both. If you clean this one up, I'll sort out Sandy and then we'll see what Mrs Mitchell has to say about it.'

In Mrs Mitchell's office, Paul refused to say a word, which left Sandy plenty of opportunity to put all the blame on him. After hearing the story, Mrs Mitchell looked thoughtfully at both boys.

'No one seems to know what started all this,' she said, 'so on this occasion I will let you go with a warning. If there is any more of this sort of behaviour, the boys involved will not take part in the sports. Do you understand? Now go and sit in your classroom for the rest of the lunch break.'

'Yes, Mrs Mitchell,' muttered the two boys and they shuffled out of the office, glaring at each other.

When the bell went, the rest of the class filed in and there was R.A., looking more self-satisfied than ever. He just couldn't stand it. As Rebecca came level with Paul's desk she was talking to her friend Carol behind her and did not notice Paul's leg shoot out. Down she fell with a mighty crash, knocking over a table as she sprawled across the floor. Her face was flushed with pain as her friends hauled her to her feet and examined her for injury. Apart from a bruised cheek she seemed unhurt, but the look she threw Paul was scorching. She knew what had happened all right!

'However did that happen, Rebecca?' asked Miss Shaw.

'I tripped,' answered Rebecca, glaring at Paul.

'Well, if there are no bones broken, just sit down.'

By the end of school that afternoon, Rebecca Allen had quite an impressive black eye and Paul kept well clear of her house on the way home. It wouldn't hurt to be a little cautious.

'What a difference from yesterday afternoon!' he thought. At home he turned the television on and watched all the programmes until Dad arrived home with two packets of fish and chips.

'Good day at school?' asked Dad vaguely.

'Yes, great!' lied Paul, and together he and Dad finished their meal. A movement outside the window caught Paul's eye and his stomach sank as he saw Rebecca Allen's father open the gate and walk towards the front door. So she had told tales, had she? He decided not to hang around to face the music and slipped out of the back door. He crouched at the front corner of the house where he could hear everything and be ready for a quick getaway. Mr Allen cleared his throat before pressing the bell. As his dad answered the door, Paul leaned forward to listen.

'I hope you don't mind me calling,' began Mr Allen, 'but I, er, believe, er, that you are having a spot of family trouble. My wife and I would be glad to help, if there is anything we can do.' Paul could hardly believe his ears. Nothing at all had been said about Rebecca's black eye. Not a word! Then he realised his dad was furious.

'I don't know who told you anything of the sort,' he shouted at Mr Allen, his voice gradually rising, 'but if people in this road minded their own business instead of poking their noses into other people's, we'd all be a lot better off!' And he slammed the door in Mr Allen's face so firmly that the letter box rattled indignantly for a few seconds. Paul rushed back into the house.

'Nosey busybody!' Dad muttered. 'Who does he think he is? As if it isn't bad enough to work in the same factory

14

with him, he has to come poking around here at night.'

'You work with him?' asked Paul in amazement.

'Yes, and a right nuisance he is, too. Always works too hard and we have to keep up with him, or the boss notices. He's a bit religious as well. Oh yes, he's a real nut, that one!'

'I can't stand Rebecca Allen, either,' said Paul. 'She's in my class at school and she's a real teacher's pet.'

Father and son looked at each other sympathetically. Here was something they had in common.

'Always look after number one, son. Never mind the rest and you'll be all right. Who needs anyone else round here, eh?'

As the days passed, Paul and his dad fell into some kind of routine at home. At school he was very careful to avoid trouble, remembering Mrs Mitchell's warning. Whenever her whistle shrilled out above the playground noise, it was not Paul who was called to her office. He tried hard in class, for he had found that it stopped his mind wandering to Mum and Katy and he had vowed never to love them again. P.E. lessons were his great joy and he could hardly wait for them each day. If the weather was fair the class would go out on the field, practising the different races for their year.

There was, of course, a straight running race which would be much further than last year, but quite within Paul's range. There was also a hurdle race and there would be a third event, usually some kind of obstacle race – there was great curiosity as to what it would be. One Friday morning, about three weeks before Sports Afternoon, Miss Shaw put them out of their misery.

'Our race this year is to be a three-legged race, so during lunch-time I would like you to find a partner.'

Paul made a dash for Sandy Graham. They were friends again after a few sweets had been exchanged at break times.

'Sandy, will you be my partner?' he asked hopefully. Sandy did not wish to appear too thrilled at being asked, but he knew he would stand a very good chance of winning with Paul as his partner.

'Oh, all right then, if you want.' And the deal was made.

By that afternoon, most children had made their choice and were standing in pairs. The few who were left over were soon sorted out, but there was an extra girl.

'All of you will have a turn,' said Miss Shaw, 'it just means that Jean will run twice with a different partner.'

Paul couldn't resist looking to see who Rebecca Allen was paired with and he felt quite sorry for Jean, who looked rather disappointed herself.

Pairs of legs were soon joined together and Miss Shaw suggested that they all walk round slowly until they felt ready to run. Along with the others, Paul and Sandy grasped each other firmly round the waist and set off, only to discover they had started on the wrong foot and collapsed in a heap. There was great opportunity for clowning around while trying to get up again and soon Miss Shaw's whistle brought order to the chaos.

'Now, then,' she said, smiling, 'I think that will be enough practising. Let's try a race or two!' And she divided them up into two groups, pairs of boys and girls in each. Paul and Sandy went off in the first group, but they had not gone ten steps before they were tripping over each other.

'I see why we have to practise,' said Paul, ruefully rubbing his shin where Sandy's elbow had landed.

But if Paul thought his effort was poor, then Rebecca's was abysmal. There was no way she and Jean were going to cross the finishing line before the end of school, the rate they were going.

'Miss Shaw,' wailed Jean, 'it's not fair! Rebecca's hopeless!'

'Now, Jean,' said their teacher, 'we all need lots of

practice. There's no need to criticise Rebecca.'

'Miss Shaw!' Now it was Rebecca speaking, flushed and looking worried. 'Please, Miss Shaw, it isn't fair for Jean to run again with me. As there's an extra girl I don't mind missing this race altogether – really I don't.'

'I'll think about it,' was all Miss Shaw said, before marshalling them to go back to the classroom.

Reaching home that afternoon, Paul vaulted over the low wall – something he had been perfecting all week – and with a grin of satisfaction he sauntered into the kitchen. After a snack to stave off the pangs of hunger until Dad came in, he wandered into the garden and played about with a football. Soon Dad arrived with a Chinese meal from the shop in town and they forked rice and bean-sprouts on to their plates before going through to eat it in front of the television. It crossed Paul's mind that Mum had never let him do that and he felt rather grown-up.

After tea, Dad announced that the grass needed cutting. There wasn't much of it and Paul went round the edges with the shears. There were a couple of steps up to the lawn and Dad heaved at the old lawnmower to drag it up them. Suddenly, he grunted and dropped the mower handle. He grabbed at his back and sat down heavily on the steps.

'What have you done, Dad? Get up, come on!'

'Leave me be, Paul! I think I've pulled a muscle. It'll be all right in a minute or two.' So Paul sat down beside him, twisting a screw on the shears and wondering what to do.

Presently, Dad pushed himself up and, leaning on Paul, managed to stagger to the kitchen door.

'This is just like the three-legged race,' cracked Paul.

'Yes, yes, very funny!' said Dad, but he seemed more than anxious to sit down in a chair.

'Look, son!' he said, 'I'm not going to be much good for anything this evening. I think you had better just go to bed.'

It was far too early to go to sleep and Paul was sorting through a pile of old comics in his room when he heard Dad call his name.

'Yes, Dad?' he answered, trying to sound sleepy.

'Can you come down?' – and there was something in the tone of his dad's voice that made Paul go straight down to the kitchen. He was sitting there where Paul had left him, his face very white. He didn't seem to notice that Paul was not in his pyjamas.

'Son, I think you're going to have to phone the doctor for me. I can't get off the chair. He'll have to give me something to stop the pain. The number is on that list by the telephone. Just tell him who you are and what has happened.'

Paul took a deep breath and went into the hall. How he wished that Mum was there! Then he pushed the thought from his mind and concentrated on dialling the doctor's number correctly. He explained what was wrong and was relieved when the doctor said he would be round as soon as he could.

It seemed no time at all before Paul opened the front door to Dr Jamieson and led him through to the kitchen.

'Off you go outside a minute,' said Dad. The doctor shut the back door and Paul was left to kick a ball against the dustbin, his eye on the front door so that he would know when the doctor left. But it was the kitchen door that opened and Paul was called inside.

'Sit down, Paul!' said Dr Jamieson. 'Now then, your Dad has got what we call a slipped disc in his back. That means that a small piece has moved out of its proper place. Sometimes, rest in bed will put it right, but your Dad is going to need some weights on his legs to straighten his back. He will probably need to be in hospital for a couple of weeks.'

'Hospital!' gasped Paul. 'What about some pills, Dad?'

'Sorry, son,' murmured Dad. 'I can't help it. I'll have to go.'

'Now, Paul,' – the doctor was speaking again and Paul looked at him in a daze. 'Your Dad tells me that you have no relations living nearby who could look after you so, with his permission, I have rung up some people whom I thought would be able to help and they are quite happy to do so. In fact, it turns out that they have a daughter in your class at school.'

Paul looked at Dr Jamieson with dawning horror as he continued, 'So Mr Allen will be round in a few minutes to fetch you. Off you go and put some pyjamas and a toothbrush in a bag!'

Paul glared at Dad. How could he? How could he let the Allens take him to their house? But Dad was past caring about anything except getting rid of the pain in his back. Paul flew upstairs and packed a carrier bag. Just as he turned to leave his bedroom, his eye caught a flash of red. It was one of Katy's little slippers pushed under his bed. Mum must have left it by mistake. Hurriedly, he stuffed it in the bag with his pyjamas and went downstairs.

Already Mr Allen had arrived. The ambulance came next and as Dad was carried out to it, he glanced absently at Paul.

'Be a good lad for me!' he said, before he was whisked away.

'I'll lock up the house,' said Mr Allen, as Dr Jamieson drove away, too.

Paul waited in the garden. Finally, the door was shut and locked and Paul walked sadly down the path behind Mr Allen.

3

Rebecca Allen lived only a dozen doors away from Paul and all too soon he found himself turning in at the gate of a house very like his own.

'Come on in, Paul,' said Mr Allen. 'I'm afraid Becky is already asleep so you won't have her company this evening.'

It took Paul a moment to realise who Becky was. He had never heard her called that before. But he was glad she was in bed. He had already decided to have as little as possible to do with R.A.

Mr Allen opened the kitchen door and a bundle of fur hurtled out.

'Get down, Ruff! Come and meet our visitor!' Paul found himself being thoroughly sniffed by a friendly, woolly sort of dog. As he bent down to stroke him, Ruff promptly rolled on the floor, waving all four legs in the air. Paul was tickling a very pleased Ruff when Mrs Allen came downstairs.

'Hello, Paul!' she said. 'I see you've made a friend already. It's quite late, but I thought you'd like some toast and a drink before bed. Do you like hot chocolate? Good!' Mrs Allen was organising him at a great rate and he soon found himself following her upstairs.

'You can have the spare room. Here's the bathroom. Will you be all right now? I'll be back in a few minutes.' And off she went downstairs.

Paul changed as quickly as he could and climbed into bed, pretending to be asleep when Mrs Allen came into his room a few minutes later. He heard her walk across the room and stand by his bed. Then the floor creaked as she tip-toed out. Paul turned over and noticed something in his bag. He leaned out of bed and pulled out Katy's little red slipper. Suddenly, that was the last straw. Flinging himself on the pillow, he sobbed as if his heart would break.

Half-way down the stairs, Mrs Allen paused as she heard the muffled crying and turned to go back to the bedroom. Then she stopped and instead, clicked her fingers to Ruff who was waiting for her at the bottom of the stairs.

'Come on, boy!' she whispered. Ruff, who was not usually allowed upstairs, needed no second invitation and bounded upwards. Mrs Allen quietly pushed open the door of Paul's room and Ruff padded in. Presently, Paul felt a cold, wet nose being pushed under his hand and a cuddly little body wriggling next to him enthusiastically. Ruff, so pleased to be on a comfortable bed, did not seem to mind that for a while his fur was wet from tears.

Worn out by all the events of the previous evening, Paul slept late on Saturday morning and it was nearly nine o'clock before he woke up. He looked round the room, and remembered where he was. For a few moments he lay still, wondering how he was going to manage to live in the same house as R.A. His father had said that Mr Allen was a bit odd, so perhaps he had better steer clear of him as well. If he *had* to stay here, there was no need to be in the house any longer than was absolutely necessary. He had just made this decision when Mrs Allen popped her head round the door.

'Ah, you're awake then! Breakfast's ready when you are!'

While Paul washed in the bathroom, he wondered whether he ought to ignore Mrs Allen as well. His mum had once said that Mrs Allen was the only neighbour who ever talked to her, but all the same, she was R.A.'s mum and would, of course, take her side against him.

Somewhat cautiously, Paul wandered downstairs and into the kitchen. There was breakfast on the table for him. Mrs Allen was busy rolling out some pastry.

'There you are!' she said, turning to smile at him. 'You sit down and eat that and we'll see what to do next.'

Ruff immediately came to lie at Paul's feet, ready for any crumbs which might fall. It was very quiet. Mrs Allen busied herself at the cooker, then after a while wiped her hands on a cloth and sat down.

'I'll have a cuppa with you,' she said. 'Becky's Dad has taken her to her piano lesson, but they'll be back later on. Is there anything you would like to do today?'

Paul grunted that there wasn't and kept his eyes on the table.

'Well then, I'm sure we can find something for you to do until visiting time.'

Paul looked up questioningly, his eyes wide open.

'Yes, of course,' smiled Mrs Allen. 'I'll take you to the hospital to see your Dad this afternoon.'

Somehow, Paul had not thought of that. He had felt that his dad had gone, like Mum. Now, here was Mrs Allen saying that he could go and see him.

'Oh, great!' he breathed. Then he suddenly remembered to be careful and looked down at his plate again.

'Now,' she said, pushing her chair back, 'how do you fancy taking Ruff for a walk? Or perhaps a run!'

Paul looked up in time to catch the twinkle in Mrs Allen's eye.

'Yes, I know you like running,' she said. 'I often see you in the early morning – almost as if you are in training!' and she winked at him.

That puzzled Paul. There was no time to work it out though, as he found himself being shown how to fasten Ruff's lead. Ruff virtually dragged him to the door in his desperation to get out and away they ran. It took Paul a while to get used to running with Ruff on the lead, but it was exciting. He had always wanted a dog and Ruff seemed to like him. He ran as hard as he could, Ruff's short legs hardly touching the ground as he raced beside Paul. They both needed a rest by the swings and Paul decided he would walk back to the house. He was dreading the meeting with Rebecca and wanted to put it off as long as possible. The conversation that was taking place in the Allen's house that very moment would have surprised him, for Mrs Allen was explaining to her daughter that Paul was lonely and unhappy and that she should do all she could to make him welcome.

'But Mum, he can't stand me!' wailed Becky.

'No matter,' said her mum. 'He is in trouble and we must care for him. Now, I am trusting you to do all you can to make it easy for him to be here.'

As Becky continued to look doubtful, her mum gave her a big hug.

'It's all a question of love,' Mum said. 'Now, what about playing your new piece on the piano?'

As Paul and Ruff came up the path a few minutes later, the sound of the piano told him that R.A. was at home. There was no escape. He would have to meet her. Perhaps if he slipped Ruff into the house he could play in the garden. But Mrs Allen had spotted him.

'Hello, Paul! Had a good run? Ruff looks as if he has! There's a drink on the table for you and Becky and I'm just taking some biscuits out of the oven. Becky!'

Before he could take evasive action, Paul found himself face to face with the detested R.A.

'Hello!' she said, tentatively.

'Hello!' growled Paul, his eyes on the ground. Then he sat down and gulped his drink. It was great, though, to taste the warm biscuits and he chewed them slowly while stroking Ruff to avoid having to look at Rebecca. When Mrs Allen went to hang out the washing, there was complete silence in the kitchen. Eventually, Rebecca took a deep breath.

'I'm sorry about your dad,' she said.

Paul's head shot up. 'Well you needn't be!' he shouted. 'I can do without your sympathy, snooty teacher's pet! I didn't want to come and stay here, so keep away from me, do you hear?'

Becky looked furious and opened her mouth to reply, but Paul never found out what she was going to say, for Mr Allen chose that moment to come into the kitchen.

'I wonder if one of you children would like to help me clean the car?' he said – and was amazed at the speed with which Paul leapt to his feet. Anything was better than sitting with R.A. and it would help to pass the rest of the morning. Lunch was a rather strained affair, with no conversation from either Becky or Paul, so Paul was relieved when Mrs Allen told him to get ready to go to hospital.

'Is there anything your dad likes to read?' she asked as they were leaving the house.

'Not really,' said Paul, 'just the newspaper and those word puzzle books.'

'Right then, let's go!'

On the way to the hospital they stopped once at a newsagent's shop and Mrs Allen sent Paul in with some money to buy a paper and a new puzzle book. When they pulled into the hospital car park, Paul began to feel uneasy. He had never been inside a hospital and wasn't at all sure it was something he was going to like. Mrs Allen led the way to an office marked 'Enquiries' and soon they were on their way along corridors and up in a lift to Ward 7.

'Ah, here it is at last!' said Mrs Allen thankfully, as she pushed open the swing doors and they went across to Mr Walker's bed.

'How are you? Do you need anything from the hospital shop?' asked Mrs Allen and soon she was off down the ward and Paul was left alone with his dad.

'Can't you get out of bed at all?' he asked, eyeing the pulleys and weights at the end of the bed.

'Not for a week, they say, and a right nuisance it is, too,' answered Dad. 'How are you getting on, son?'

'Not too badly,' said Paul. 'I've decided to say as little as possible and I should think that Rebecca will do the same. Mrs Allen's OK though.'

'Yes, she seems friendly enough,' agreed his dad. 'Strange people, the Allens, though. I mean, he works with me and yet he seems to know all sorts of people quite well. Perhaps he's in some club or other.'

Then he changed the subject abruptly. 'Are these papers for me, or are you keeping them warm?'

'Oh, I forgot,' laughed Paul, and handed them over.

Paul wasn't sure what to talk about after that and was pleased when Mrs Allen returned with her purchases. As Dad was sorting money from his wallet, the bell went, announcing the end of visiting time.

'Cheerio, son!' called Dad. 'Come again, eh?'

'Yes, of course he will,' smiled Mrs Allen as they left.

Once outside the ward, Paul felt lonely and was glad that Mrs Allen was too busy finding the way out of the hospital to talk to him. It was tea-time when they arrived back at the house and when it was over, Mr Allen suggested a walk. At the word 'walk', Ruff went into a frenzy of excitement, barking and dancing around on his hind legs. Paul had to laugh as Mr Allen struggled to fasten the lead, but eventually Ruff was attached and calmed down a little.

'Want to come?' Mr Allen asked Paul.

'Er, I don't think so . . .' began Paul, but Ruff had other ideas. Leaping up, he caught Paul's sleeve in his mouth and pulled him off the chair.

'All right, all right, I'll come!' laughed Paul, disengaging himself from Ruff's mouth.

'You'd better have the lead,' said Mr Allen. 'Ruff has certainly taken a fancy to you.'

Mr Allen showed Paul parts of the town that he had never seen before. There were several footpaths which would be good for running practice, Paul decided, although they were rather far from home. Then they passed an athletics club.

'That's quite a good club,' said Mr Allen.

'Aha,' thought Paul, 'So that's the club he belongs to, is it?'

But Mr Allen went on, 'I'm not a member myself, but I've heard other people speak highly of it. I think there's a junior club, too. Perhaps they have some information about it,' and he disappeared through a door.

'Whatever has he done that for?' wondered Paul as he waited outside. 'Rebecca Allen would scarcely enjoy an athletics club!'

But when Mr Allen came out with some leaflets he said: 'They have some vacancies at the moment and they said boys are always welcome.'

Paul was struck dumb. It had been for him that Mr Allen had been enquiring – not Becky.

'Perhaps your dad would be interested in these,' continued Mr Allen showing Paul the leaflets.

'Oh, no, I shouldn't think so,' replied Paul. 'You'd better keep them.'

The walk home seemed much shorter, possibly because Ruff pulled at the lead, anxious to have the dog biscuits which he knew he would find in his bowl. After a quick drink, Paul announced that he was rather tired and would go to bed. He reckoned that he had had enough of the Allens for one day.

4

Next morning, a shock awaited Paul. After breakfast, Mr Allen mentioned casually that they'd be leaving for church in half an hour. Paul was thunderstruck. Church? He had never been there! That was only for snobs, cissies and religious nuts, his dad had always said. Mrs Allen took one look at his face and asked: 'Are you not used to going, Paul?'

'Er, no, not really,' stammered Paul, desperately looking for an excuse not to go.

'How about coming this once?' suggested Mrs Allen. 'We're all going, as it's Family Service. I'll tell you what! We'll sit right at the back and if you really don't like it, we'll come out.'

And so it was settled. Half an hour later Paul followed the Allens, rather uneasily, into the church building he had often run past. Before today, he had never given it another thought.

It was strangely quiet and cool. An elderly gentleman near the door gave them each two books and, true to her word, Mrs Allen led the way into a row of seats at the very back, nearest the door. There didn't appear to be many people in the church, but Paul guessed they were early. He couldn't help looking round with fascination at the huge blocks of stone which made up the arches and pillars. On the walls there were plaques with the names of people who had died, and above those were beautifully coloured stained glass windows, each one with a different picture. Strange that he hadn't noticed them from outside. He was glad that Rebecca was on the other side of her parents. It would be more than flesh and blood could bear to have to sit next to her.

More people began to come in and he glanced at them idly to see what sort of an odd bunch they would be. He was startled to see one of the teachers from school and the policeman who came to give them road safety lectures. There were old people, young people, children – even a couple of prams were pushed in. Paul was hardly surprised when Dr Jamieson came in. He caught sight of the Allens and came over.

'Hello, John!' he said, shaking Mr Allen's hand. 'Good to see you, Rosemary, Becky,' and he nodded at Mrs Allen and Rebecca. 'Hello, Paul – how's things?'

'All right,' mumbled Paul, and Dr Jamieson glanced quickly at Mr Allen.

'We'll be in touch, Peter,' said Mr Allen, before the doctor went off to find a seat nearer the front.

This must be the club that Dad was talking about, for there were certainly a lot of people who greeted the Allens as if they knew them very well indeed. They didn't seem to be the odd people that Dad had told him went to church. They were all quite ordinary. It was rather disappointing.

The service began and, in spite of himself, Paul did enjoy the singing which was loud and reverberated round the church. The rest of what happened was a bit of a mystery, though. Everyone else knew where to read in the other book – not the hymn book – and although Mrs Allen found the place for him, he didn't bother to follow the words.

Eventually, a man in a long white robe, with a black scarf over it, stood up in the pulpit. Paul assumed that this was the vicar. He'd seen them on television. The vicar began to tell a story of a man who had been attacked and of two people who left him lying there; and of another man, a supposed enemy, who took care of him. The vicar then asked if any of the children could tell him which of the three had been a friend to the injured man. Paul thought that was pretty obvious and decided not to listen any more when the vicar began to talk about other things.

At the end of the service, Paul slipped out and waited in the car park. There was no need to be noticed by too many people. The Allens were chatting to everyone – or so it appeared to Paul – but eventually Mr Allen saw Paul and came to open the car, before rounding up his wife and Becky.

Ruff was pleased to see them all when they reached home and Paul made a fuss of him to avoid having to talk to anyone. After lunch, it was time to visit Dad again. Mrs Allen spent much of the time talking to another patient who had no visitors. When he was sure that Mrs Allen was out of earshot, Paul leaned over the bed.

'Hey, Dad,' he whispered, 'you'll never guess. I went to church!'

'You what?' exclaimed Dad.

'Keep your voice down, Dad, I don't want Mrs Allen to hear,' went on Paul. 'Don't worry, I didn't listen, but I thought you'd like to know how Mr Allen knows so many people. They're all at his church. Oh, yes, and Dr Jamieson and Mr Allen were like old friends. Why don't we have lots of friends, Dad?'

'Because we mind our own business, that's why, son. Remember what I told you, always look after number one! I'm not sure you ought to go to church. Perhaps I'd better speak to Mrs Allen.' Dad paused. 'On second thoughts,' he said, 'they *are* looking after you and it wouldn't do to spoil that, would it? I suppose it won't do any harm a couple of times,' and he grinned. 'It'll be something to laugh about when I get out of here.'

In bed that night, Paul found his mind was occupied with a very pressing problem – how to get to school the next morning. There was no way that he was going to walk into the playground with R.A.! That would really give the boys something to laugh at. Finally, he came up with what he thought was a satisfactory solution. If he had his running practice after breakfast, instead of before, he could arrive at school from the opposite direction and no one would suspect anything.

Monday morning came and with it every rain-filled cloud in the area. As soon as Paul woke up he could hear the rain lashing against his bedroom window. He rushed to look out and realised there was no chance of it stopping before school time. With horror he looked at the ever-enlarging puddles and the streams of water gushing along in the gutters and down the drains. Waiting until he heard Rebecca practising the piano, he dawdled downstairs.

'What a morning!' said Mr Allen from the kitchen doorway. 'Never mind! I'll run you and Becky to school in the car.'

Paul managed to grunt, 'Thanks,' but his tone of voice was anything but grateful.

'I'm afraid you'll be a bit early, but I should think you'll be able to go right into school on a morning like this,' continued Mrs Allen.

A sigh of relief broke from Paul. None of his friends was ever early.

Becky joined him for breakfast and after sultry 'Hellos' on both sides, they ate in silence. It was indeed early when they piled into the car and went the half mile or so to the school. Paul was out of the car like a shot as soon as it came to a standstill. By the time R.A. arrived in the cloakroom, Paul was already sitting at his desk.

'Success!' thought Paul. He was pretty sure that R.A. wouldn't be telling anyone. His secret was safe – or so he thought!

Half-way through maths, Paul began to realise that some of his friends were whispering to each other. They always stopped guiltily when he spun round to look at them. Eventually, he noticed that a grubby piece of paper was being passed round. When it passed behind him, he whipped round and snatched it. He read the little note and, clenching his fists, turned to scowl at his friends. They were thoroughly enjoying his embarrassment. Paul looked back at the note. 'Paul Walker loves Rebecca Allen' was all it said, but that was enough! He crunched the piece of paper into a tiny ball. As Miss Shaw was busy with a group at the other side of the room, the rest of the gang made rude faces at him and sniggered mercilessly. By the end of the morning various threats had been issued and, had the class been allowed outside at lunch-time, the matter would have been settled there and then. The rain put paid to that and it was four o'clock before justice could be done. Paul stayed as long as he dared in the cloakroom but, late as he was, there was the gang waiting for him.

'Who's got a girl-friend, then?' they called as he drew level with them.

'Who likes teacher's pet? Who comes to school in her car?' They followed him down the path, teasing and laughing at him. Paul suddenly swung his bag round in a full circle, hitting one or two boys on the way. That was the signal. The others leapt on top of Paul, raring for a good fight. But with four boys to one, the fight was anything but good for Paul. Vaguely, he remembered Mrs Mitchell's threat, but honour had to be upheld. Nobody teased Paul Walker and got away with it.

Becky had stayed behind to help clear up after painting and as she left school she saw, at the end of the path, what appeared to be a writhing heap of arms and legs. She was turning to go down the other track when she recognised the blue and white stripes of Paul's anorak. He was at the bottom of the heap of bodies and was definitely getting the worst of it.

'Serves him right!' she said to herself. Then she remembered what Mum had said. She also remembered that in the story at church, it had been a supposed enemy of the

31

injured man who had helped him.

'That's all very well,' thought Rebecca, 'but it wouldn't do any good if I tried to stop them. I'd only get hurt myself.'

She thrust her hands deep into her pockets and turned away, but as she did so, her fingers closed around something and she quickly drew it out. It was the whistle she always carried when she went fell-walking with Mum and Dad on her holidays. Quick as a flash, she ducked round the corner of a classroom and blew a loud blast. The effect was devastating! In an instant the boys scattered, running away in all directions. Becky peeped round the corner in time to see Paul retrieving his bag from the litter bin before taking to his heels.

Becky was amazed at her own audacity as she pocketed the whistle and set off for home. Paul was up in the bathroom and when he emerged, most of the dirt and signs of the scuffle were gone, apart from a couple of bruises and a torn pocket. The children passed each other on the stairs, but each looked the other way. Becky hugged her little secret to herself. She had helped Paul and he didn't even know it. Nor would she ever tell him!

Paul's main worry next day was that at any minute Mrs Mitchell was going to send for him and ban him from the sports. That whistle blast must have been hers. But the day wore on and no summons came. Still, he was afraid to risk another fight and he knew that the rest of the gang would be wanting to finish what they had started. So he stayed behind that evening to help sort out the library corner and when he finally left school, he decided to cut across the field and jump the fence. But the gang was waiting and he was spotted. He ran as hard as he could, but they caught up with him as he was climbing the fence and brought him to the ground with a thud. He started to defend himself when once again the loud shrill of a whistle resounded over the field. Again, the effect was instant!

Without even looking round to see who was there, each boy took off across the field – Paul included. However, the whistle blower was not so fortunate. Becky had been behind some bushes, waiting for Paul to leave school. As she pushed her way on to the path, she slipped and fell full length into a patch of mud. It was a long walk home after that and when she arrived in the kitchen, Paul gasped with surprise.

'Oh, Becky!' exclaimed Mrs Allen. 'Just look at the state you're in! And you're late. You knew that I wanted tea early so that we could get to hospital promptly. It's too bad!'

Becky looked decidedly unhappy. Paul sat feeling smug.

'Now, give me that anorak,' said Mrs Allen, sharply. 'It will have to be washed. Have you no sense, Becky? It's not like you to dawdle.'

With that, Mrs Allen took the anorak and began emptying the pockets on to the table.

'No, don't Mum . . .' gabbled Becky, but it was too late. Out came paper hankies, half a packet of sweets – and one shiny metal whistle.

'There now, put those away while I put this in the washing machine,' said Mrs Allen, too busy to notice that her daughter's face had turned a deep shade of red. The smirk disappeared from Paul's face.

'Now, I'm going to your house to find some more pyjamas for your dad, Paul. I'll be back in a minute,' and Mrs Allen went out, oblivious of the questions that were hanging unspoken in the air.

After the kitchen door shut there was silence. Neither of them moved. Then Paul said very quietly: 'Is that your whistle?'

'Yes, Dad gave it to me when we went walking on holiday.'

'It looks like a teacher's whistle.'

'Yes, doesn't it?' agreed Becky, looking at her feet.

'Someone blew a whistle yesterday and today to stop a fight I was in,' said Paul, casually.

'Did they?' said Becky, shrugging carelessly.

'Was it you, then?' demanded Paul. Becky raised her head defiantly and looked directly at Paul.

'Yes, it was me. And what are you going to do about it?'

Paul was stuck for words. He stared at this strange girl who didn't like him and yet had got herself into trouble because of him. He picked up the whistle and turned it over in his hands. Then he glanced at Becky again.

'Er, thanks!' he said and pushed the whistle back across the table. Becky's face flushed again, but this time it was with pleasure. She felt as if a great weight had lifted off her shoulders.

5

Later that evening, when Paul returned home from visiting his dad, it became obvious to Mr and Mrs Allen that something was different. Becky was in the kitchen and made no attempt to rush upstairs. When she shyly offered Paul a drink, her mum and dad exchanged looks of astonishment before leaving the room.

'I've been thinking about tomorrow afternoon,' ventured Becky. 'After tonight, I daren't be late again. D'you think that the gang would do anything if you walked home with me?'

Paul almost choked. Speaking to R.A. was one thing, but to walk home with her . . .!

'Er, well, I don't think . . .' he stammered.

'You mean you're afraid of what they'll say,' said Becky.

'No . . . well, yes . . . oh, what does it matter! I *will* walk home with you. In fact,' said Paul, throwing caution to the winds, 'I'll even walk you there in the morning!'

The next day dawned fine and clear and Mrs Allen was pleased, if a little puzzled, to see Paul and Becky set off to school together. They did not talk much, as each was scanning the road ahead for any sign of trouble.

It was not until they turned the last corner before school that they saw two of the gang walking towards the gate from the opposite direction. Paul began to whistle nonchalantly and Becky became intensely interested in the hedge she was passing. Out of the corner of her eye, she could see that the two boys had stopped and were staring open-mouthed at the sight of their respected leader walking with a girl. And Rebecca Allen, at that! Fortunately, Paul and Becky had timed their journey so that they arrived as the bell rang, so Steve and John had no time to say anything.

During the first part of the morning, Paul received some very odd looks but he took no notice and worked as hard as he could. Every now and then, when she was sure no one else was looking, Becky gave him a conspiratorial wink and he nodded back. At morning break, Paul found himself surrounded by the gang, not daring to fight within sight of the playground attendant, but certainly prepared to tease the life out of Paul. Oddly, though, whatever they said to him had no effect. He simply smiled and waited until they had finished.

'I'd like to show you something that R.A. usually carries in her pocket,' he said, and produced the whistle.

'Well, what of it?' asked Sandy, scornfully.

'Just that I wondered if you'd ever heard her blowing it – that was all.' Paul raised his eyebrows and looked at each of them in turn.

For a few moments the boys were puzzled then one by one they realised that they had all run away from Rebecca Allen – not once, but twice! Their mocking changed to indignation.

'That's not fair. I'll get her for that!' threatened Steve.

'You lay a finger on her and I'll make sure that everyone knows that you ran away from a girl,' said Paul quietly.

Paul's friends looked at him in amazement. He was serious! Their stunned silence gave Paul the opportunity to do some explaining.

'Look, my dad's in hospital and the doctor fixed me up at the Allens so, like it or not, I have to stay there. R.A.'s really not so bad – for a girl – so you'll have to get used to it.'

The boys remained silent. Their leader had gone off his head. Then Sandy came and stood in front of Paul.

'You can forget the three-legged race,' he said. 'I don't run with traitors.' With that he turned on his heel and marched off, the other three scurrying along behind him.

Back in the classroom, Miss Shaw announced that they would have sports practice until lunch-time.

'Great!' thought Paul, then noticed Sandy limping out to the front.

'I seem to have hurt my foot at break, Miss Shaw,' he lied. 'May I be excused sports practice?'

'Very well,' said Miss Shaw, 'you can stay in the classroom and get on with your project work.'

That wasn't quite what Sandy had expected, but it did mean that Paul wouldn't run with him in the three-legged race that day.

'Have a go with someone else, Paul,' suggested Miss Shaw.

'No thanks,' he replied, 'I've been practising with Sandy. I'll just watch.'

Miss Shaw had decided that pairs of boys and girls could race against each other in the three-legged race and the girls came in ahead of the boys almost every time – with one notable exception. Becky and Jean barely reached half-way before the race was over. Strangely, Paul did not gain any pleasure from that today. Instead, he felt a little sorry for Becky. At least when he failed at schoolwork Miss Shaw was the only one who knew about it. Out here on Sports Afternoon, everyone would see Becky tripping over her own feet, for Miss Shaw had decided that she ought to take part.

As Becky and Paul left school that afternoon, they knew they were being watched. However, the gang did not bother them. They had taken Paul's threat seriously and did not want to spoil their image, even if Paul was ruining his. On the way home, Paul began to talk about the sports.

'I want to win everything,' he said. 'That will show them!'

'If only I could run like you,' said Becky, wistfully.

Paul stopped in his tracks.

'You mean, you want to?' he asked. 'You're so good at everything else, I thought you probably didn't care.'

'Well I do!' retorted Becky. 'I don't want to win, or anything like that. I'd just rather not feel like a baby elephant with clogs on. Honestly, I hate P.E.'

'And there I was thinking you were so happy and smug,' said Paul, thoughtfully. 'Why, I think you are as jealous of me as I am of you.'

'Oh dear,' sighed Becky, her brow wrinkling, 'I'm sure we're not supposed to be jealous, but I can't help it. I do so want Dad and Mum to be pleased with me at sports.'

They walked on, both deep in thought. Suddenly, Paul turned to Becky.

'Look, seeing you got me out of trouble, how about me teaching you to run a bit better?'

'Would you?' breathed Becky, 'I will try, really I will. When shall we start?'

'How about tonight?' he suggested.

'Great!' said Becky. 'We'll start after tea. You know, to make things fair, I really ought to teach you something.'

'There is something,' said Paul, 'but you must promise not to tell anybody.'

'I promise,' said Becky solemnly, wondering what awful thing it could be.

'Don't laugh, but I always wanted to play the recorder. When the letter came home about it, Dad said that he didn't want that noise around the house and wouldn't let me do it. You couldn't show me how to play, could you?

Becky was relieved that the request was not a difficult one.

'I'm sure I could teach you the first few lessons,' she said. 'The book is very clear. You can use my recorder.'

'Down at the shed?' suggested Paul.

'Down at the shed,' agreed Becky.

They had arrived at Becky's house and went in, chatting like old friends. Mrs Allen thought she would never cease to wonder at childhood friendships. One minute they were sworn enemies, the next the best of friends. If children could learn to get on with each other, she mused, then perhaps grown-ups could, too. Mrs Walker, Paul's mum, had talked to her a few times. She had been so unhappy that it had not really surprised Mrs Allen when she had heard that Mrs Walker had gone away, but it made her very sad.

Down in the shed, Paul and Becky were busy making plans. Paul was describing to Becky the importance of breathing deeply, using her arms and striding out boldly. He was an avid watcher of all the athletics programmes on television and now felt that he was very knowledgeable on the subject.

'But how do I breathe and move my arms and legs all at the same time?' asked Becky.

'You just do!' he said. 'Come on! Let's run round the block.'

'I'll pop in and tell Mum where I'm going,' said Becky. Paul waited for her at the gate.

'Right! Are you ready?' asked Paul, positioning himself for a good start.

'I think so,' came the reply.

'We'll jog to the corner and then open up along the next bit of pavement,' explained Paul.

'Open up?' enquired Becky.

'Run! I mean,' said Paul.

'Oh, of course – that kind of open up,' said Becky, wishing she were somewhere else.

'Let's go!' shouted Paul, and they set off to the corner, jogging slowly.

'This is fine!' panted Becky, before she tripped over a paving stone.

'How did you do that?' asked Paul, as he hauled her to her feet.

'Quite easily – I do it all the time.'

'Right! Let's go again,' said Paul, when Becky had brushed herself down. But by the time they had reached the corner, Becky was flushed and out of breath.

'We haven't even started running yet,' said Paul.

'Oh, no!' gasped Becky.

'Come on, run to the next corner. Now!'

They set off together, but soon Paul was streaking ahead. Becky struggled to catch him, but only succeeded in tripping herself up.

'I don't believe it!' said Paul, as he ran back to her. 'What did you fall over this time?'

'My feet!' said Becky.

Paul looked at her incredulously.

'People don't trip over their own feet,' he said.

'I do!' replied Becky.

'Let's go back to the shed and have a re-think,' suggested Paul, wondering whether he hadn't been a little rash to volunteer his coaching services.

'We'll do a bit of recorder – you might come up with some new ideas after that,' said Becky.

A few minutes later, Becky wiped the mouthpiece of her recorder and handed it to Paul. Paul was surprised that what had looked so easy when Becky had done it was so difficult when he tried. His fingers kept slipping off the holes and he was sure he wasn't doing the right things with his tongue.

'Come on,' said Becky, 'keep at it!'

'That's enough for one night,' said Paul, surveying the little circular pads on his fingers and thumb. 'Now about your running. We'll try again tomorrow night. In the meantime, practise breathing.'

'But I breathe all the time,' said Becky.

'I mean deep breathing – like this! In, two, three. Out,

two, three. In, two, three . . .' and Paul demonstrated.

'In, two, three. Out, two, three,' intoned Becky, as she walked into the kitchen.

'Anyone for tea, two, three?' laughed her dad on his way out of the kitchen.

Becky frowned. 'I think that from now on we'd better not let Dad and Mum see what we're doing. They don't realise that this is serious.'

'Quite right,' agreed Paul, 'they'll find out soon enough when you win a race at sports.'

'And you'll be playing a tune on the recorder soon,' said Becky, as she made a cup of tea for everyone.

Paul sat stroking Ruff and thinking how good it felt to be in this house. But he missed his own little Katy and, most of all, his mum. Perhaps one day he would talk to Mrs Allen about it. He was sure she would understand. Yes, he decided, at the first opportunity he was going to ask Mrs Allen some very important questions.

6

Paul had many things on his mind for the next few days. On the one hand, he was looking forward to the sports, but Mum would not be there – possibly not even Dad. He was enjoying living at the Allens' house, but he knew that wasn't going to last long. It would be good to have Dad back home, but it wouldn't be the same without Mum. There were so many 'buts'. Sometimes it was like being on a see-saw – down in the dumps one minute, up in the air the next. He did not like it.

'Do your mum and dad ever argue?' he suddenly asked Becky one afternoon on the way home.

'Oh, yes!' replied Becky.

'I've never heard them,' said Paul.

'It's usually about things like what colour to do the paintwork, or who forgot to lock the car – things like that,' said Becky.

'Those aren't rows,' said Paul. 'I meant, do they ever shout at each other?'

Becky coloured a little. 'I did once hear them getting very cross. I was supposed to be in bed.'

'What happened?' asked Paul, intently.

'I'm not sure,' replied Becky, 'but after a while I heard Dad say sorry to Mum. She said it was her fault and she was sorry, too. When I peeped downstairs, they were holding hands over the table, so I decided that it was all right.'

'I expect I'd think that too,' said Paul sadly. Then he called out: 'Race you to the corner!' and he was off.

Becky struggled along behind him for, though she was

less clumsy than she had been, running was still an effort. Paul sometimes wondered what he was achieving with Becky's coaching but, oddly enough, his own technique was improving. For his part, he was learning a new note on the recorder each night and by Friday evening he could play one of the simpler tunes in the book. Becky was very pleased.

'That's great!' she said. 'A few more weeks and you'll have caught up with all of us.'

'I'm not musical like you,' said Paul.

'Who says?' demanded Becky. 'I bet you would be if you had proper lessons.'

In fact, it was Becky's piano lesson on Saturday morning which gave Paul the opportunity he had been waiting for to speak to Mrs Allen. When Becky and her father left, Paul was finishing his breakfast in the kitchen. Mrs Allen was ironing. He fiddled with the teaspoons on the table whilst he wondered how to start. Eventually, he decided to come straight out with it.

'Mrs Allen?'

'Yes, Paul,' she replied, without turning from her ironing.

'Does my mum not love me any more?' There! He had said it at last!

Mrs Allen stood quite still for a moment, then she turned and looked at him.

'Why should you think that?' she asked.

'Well, it's obvious, isn't it?' Paul was speaking quickly. 'She went off and left Dad and me, but she took Katy – so she must love her and not me,' and tears began to prick his eyes.

Mrs Allen hesitated as if she were wondering whether or not to tell him something. Then she reached for a shirt and began to iron it before she answered.

'Do you remember what you did the night you found that your mum had gone?'

Paul thought a while. 'Well, yes. I ran and ran for ages until I was too tired and had to go home,' he said, wondering what all this had to do with Mum.

'I knew that, because I saw you go,' said Mrs Allen, 'but can you tell me why you ran?'

'I suppose I just wanted to run away.'

'Perhaps that is what your mum had to do,' she said. 'Sometimes, grown-ups get to their wits' end and the only thing they can do is run. The difference is that grown-ups usually know where to go and don't have to come back when they get hungry.'

'But why should Mum be at her wits' end?' demanded Paul. 'She had Katy and me. We both loved her. And she had Dad . . .' His voice trailed away as he remembered the rows he had heard night after night.

Mrs Allen was speaking again. 'There are times, Paul, when I have wanted to run away.'

Paul looked at her in disbelief.

'Oh, yes,' she went on. 'Mums can get very tired and lonely with no other grown-ups to talk to all day. Much as we love our children, they can drive us to distraction, sometimes,' she said, rather ruefully.

'Why didn't you run away?' asked Paul.

There was a pause while Mrs Allen carefully folded the shirt. Again it looked as if she were deciding whether or not to explain.

'Well, Paul,' she said, at last, 'when everyone else doesn't seem to care about me, or I think they don't understand, I have a friend I can talk to at any time and he shares all my problems. He loves me, too – and that helps a lot.'

'Do you mean Mr Allen?' asked Paul.

'No, I don't,' smiled Mrs Allen, 'though he does help. No, the friend that I am talking about is God.'

'Oh,' said Paul, not being able to think of anything else to say.

'You see,' went on Mrs Allen, 'I believe that God made

us all and so he is interested in each one of us. When we are sad, he cares.'

Paul had been thinking while she was talking.

'But how do you talk to God? And how does he talk to you?'

'I can talk to God any time I like – some people call it praying. When I read the Bible, I read what he is saying to me. Sometimes, things happen which show me what to do. But,' she went on, as she struggled to fold a sheet, 'that is not answering your first question. I am sure your mum does love you. I should think that it hurts her to be away from you as much as it hurts you to be left. If you think about it, she couldn't leave Katy because she's not at school. She couldn't take you with her because you would have missed school.'

Mrs Allen sounded so certain of what she was saying that, for a second, Paul wondered if she had spoken to his mum.

'Will Mum come back?' he asked quietly.

'Paul, I cannot say definitely that she will, but I have told my special friend all about it.'

'Oh,' was all Paul could say. Suddenly, he rushed across the kitchen and gave Mrs Allen a big hug.

'Please tell him that I would like her to come back,' he said in a muffled voice – then he ran out of the door, followed by Ruff.

Mrs Allen sat at the table quietly wondering if she had said the right things. What she had not told Paul was that on her afternoon visit to Mr Walker, he had given her a telephone number where Paul's mum could be contacted. She had already rung Mrs Walker to reassure her that Paul was all right.

'Please ring again,' Paul's mum had said at the end of the call. 'I do miss him so much, but I can't come back. I just can't!'

7

Paul thought that it did not seem like a week since last Sunday, but here he was again, sitting in church. Today, Becky would leave half-way through to go to Sunday School, but Paul had chosen to stay with Mr and Mrs Allen.

The service was much the same as the previous week and Paul was still a bit puzzled by the standing up and sitting down at odd times. However, this time he did not feel uncomfortable and tried to remember as much as he could to tell Dad. After quite a bit of singing and praying, a boy stood up to read.

'The New Testament lesson,' he said, 'is taken from Paul's second letter to Timothy, chapter four.'

Paul sat bolt upright. He didn't even know a Timothy, never mind writing him a letter! Then he saw that Mrs Allen was following the words in her Bible. He relaxed. It was another Paul! He had begun to count the number of stones in each pillar when the words the boy was reading made him stop and listen.

'I have done my best in the race, I have run the full distance and I have kept the faith. And now there is waiting for me the prize of victory . . .'

Paul did not listen any more. Fancy hearing about athletics in church! Wait till he told Dad that one!

The next hymn was almost as startling, for he found himself singing about running the straight race through God's good grace. He wasn't sure about the last bit, but he could certainly run a straight race. There was more to church than met the eye.

As the vicar stood up to speak, Paul wondered if there would be anything else about running. He was not disappointed, for it appeared that the Paul in the Bible had written another letter in which he talked about forgetting what was behind him and doing his best to reach what was ahead. Paul thought that was pretty sound advice and tried to remember it to tell Becky. Pity she wasn't there! The vicar seemed to stray off the subject after that and began to speak about another kind of race. The rest of the service passed quite quickly and when it was over Becky came back from Sunday School.

Dr Jamieson was standing by the door as they left.

'Hello, Paul!' he said. 'I hoped I would see you. I visited the hospital yesterday and the doctor there says that your dad can get up this week and start moving round. All being well, he may be home at the end of the week. That's good, isn't it?'

'Oh, yes!' said Paul, enthusiastically, and turned to Becky to give her the news.

Becky's reaction was not what he had expected, for she only managed to say: 'That will be nice for you,' before she walked away.

'Now, whatever is the matter with her?' he thought.

Dr Jamieson must have read his thoughts, for he said: 'Do you know, I think Becky will miss you when you go back home. I hear you have been spending a lot of time together.'

'Miss me?' said Paul, incredulously, striking his chest with his fist. 'Miss me? Phew!' and he shrugged his shoulders.

But the more Paul thought about it, the more he realised that Becky wasn't the only one who was going to feel lonely. He hadn't realised until now just how much he was enjoying staying at the Allens' house. There was something about Mr and Mrs Allen that he couldn't put his finger on. He would have to watch them this week and see what made them different. It wasn't that they were never cross, because they could be quite annoyed with Becky if she did something wrong. He just couldn't figure it out.

On the way home, Paul tried to cheer Becky up.

'There was a good piece of athletics coaching in church this morning,' he said.

'Athletics? In church?' frowned Becky.

'Well, there was a bit about running a straight race and some more about not looking behind. I was a bit surprised to hear it myself,' he added.

'Dad, what is Paul talking about?' asked Becky.

'He's quite right,' said Mr Allen. 'The Bible does talk about running a race. It says that the life of a Christian is like a long race. It has to be lived as you would run a race – always pressing forward and aiming for the very best . . .'

'See?' interrupted Paul. 'You didn't believe me, did you, Becky?'

Back at the house Paul went upstairs to read some comics. He leafed through a pile that Becky had dumped in his room, then he rolled on his back with his hands behind his head. There was something puzzling him about what Mr Allen had said – the life of a Christian is like a race. What did he mean by a Christian? But he didn't want to ask too many questions in case the Allens thought he was silly. He crossed the landing to Becky's room and tapped on the door.

'Hello, come and hear my new record,' said Becky, pulling out an old record player from under her bed.

Becky put on the record and they listened to it together for a while. Then Paul began to look along Becky's bookshelf. Most of the books were about animals or ballet dancers, but at the end he noticed a little booklet sticking out.

'What is a Christian?' read the title. Here was a chance to get his question answered without anyone knowing.

'Could I borrow some books for my room?' he asked.

'Sure!' said Becky.

Paul pulled out a few large books from the shelf and managed to slip the booklet on the bottom.

'Lunch-time!' called Mrs Allen.

The answer would have to wait. That afternoon, Paul went to visit his dad again with Mrs Allen. As they pulled into the car park, his eyes roamed along the side of the building. Dad was sitting by a window, waving!

'Look, it's Dad!' he yelled to Mrs Allen, as she got out of the car.

'Hey wait for me!' shouted Mrs Allen, as Paul rushed off to Ward 7.

'Hi, Dad! You look great! How d'you feel? Dr Jamieson says you'll be home at the end of the week!'

Paul was stumbling over his words with excitement. He realised how uncomfortable he had felt visiting Dad when he was confined to bed. He hadn't seemed like Dad at all. This was more like it, to see him sitting in a chair, poking him with mock punches.

'Slow down, son, or you'll send my blood pressure sky high,' laughed Dad. 'I feel good, but a little wobbly when I stand up. If I do all the exercises the physiotherapist gives me, they say I'll be home at the weekend.'

Mrs Allen had joined them and heard the last remark.

'Well, I'll put a few things in the fridge ready for you, so that you don't have to go shopping too soon.'

'She's all right, that one,' said Dad, as Mrs Allen went down the ward to speak to an old man who never had any visitors of his own.

'I don't suppose you have visitors when I'm at school,' said Paul, regretfully.

'Ah, well,' said Dad. 'I've had one or two, you know.'

'Oh,' said Paul, 'who?'

'Oh, er . . . well, er . . . Mr Allen has popped in a couple of times,' and Dad had a sudden fit of coughing.

'Mr Allen?' repeated Paul. 'I thought you couldn't

stand him.'

Dad looked harassed. 'Now look, son, you don't always show what you feel about people. I mean, you *are* staying at their house. I could hardly tell the man to go away when he'd taken an hour off work to come, could I?'

Paul was intrigued. 'Whatever do you talk about?'

'Oh, this and that. Nothing to interest you, although he did give me these.' Dad reached into his locker and brought out a handful of leaflets from the athletics club. Paul held his breath.

'Mr Allen seems to think that you would enjoy something like this. Would you?'

'Oh, yes,' breathed Paul.

Dad looked at him thoughtfully. 'Well,' he said at last, 'I suppose it won't do any harm to fill in the forms.'

'Oh, thanks Dad! That's terrific!' Paul beamed from ear to ear.

'Now, what have you been up to today?' asked Dad.

'We went to church again. It was all about running races.'

'Are you sure, son?' asked Dad, doubtfully.

'Yes, really! Only not our kind of race. Hey, Dad! Will you be able to come to Sports Afternoon a week on Wednesday?'

'Yes, I should think so. I've to stay off work for a week after I leave here. They're very good to you in this hospital, but I'll be glad to get home. Mind you, I've had time to sort a few things out.'

Paul hardly dared to ask, but he had to. 'What about, Dad?'

'Oh, you know,' said Dad vaguely. 'How to keep the house clean, when to do the shopping and when to go to the launderette.'

Paul's face fell. 'Oh, just that!'

'Why, what did you think I would be sorting out?' asked Dad.

'Oh, nothing,' said Paul.

Next day Paul left earlier to get a run, before meeting Becky at the school gate.

'I've been thinking,' she said, 'it's a shame you're not going to have a partner in the three-legged race. Now that James is absent Sandy's running with Alan. I mean it doesn't matter that I'm not running. I'm no good anyway.'

'Honestly,' said Paul, 'I wish you weren't so pathetic about your running. No wonder you're so bad at it! And he went into school.

Becky stood where he had left her. So that's what he really thought, was it? Well, she'd show him.

It was warm that afternoon and the children lazed under the trees at the end of the field waiting for their turn. When the first group of girls was called for the running race, Paul noticed idly that Becky was with them.

'Oh, no!' he thought. 'I don't think I can bear to look.' But he did. Becky was poised for the start.

'At least she's learned that much,' thought Paul.

Then Miss Shaw blew the whistle and they were off, hair streaming out behind them as they pounded up the field. Paul waited for the gap to open between Becky and the others. But Becky was holding her own! Paul grabbed the boy next to him who was trying to get a noise out of a piece of grass between his fingers and thumb.

'Hey, watch it!' Gary yelled. 'I nearly swallowed the grass.'

'No, you watch!' said Paul, urgently. He pointed down the field.

'What's happened to Old Foot-in-mouth?' exclaimed Gary. 'She looks as if she might not be last.'

Spurred on by a strong desire to make Paul eat his words, Becky had found that her legs would obey her. At the finishing line it was a close thing who was last, Becky or Jean.

'All right R.A.' grinned Paul as Becky walked past him. 'So you're not that bad.'

'Never thought I would see the day when she would keep up with the others,' said Gary. 'I wonder what's happened to her?'

Back in the classroom Miss Shaw continued with the rest of the afternoon's work, but Paul could no longer concentrate. He had just had the craziest idea. It involved taking a certain risk but it was better than nothing. The more he thought about it, the more excited he became. When the bell went he dawdled about at his desk until all the others had gone. Then he went forward to speak to Miss Shaw. Becky was waiting for him in the playground.

'Well?' she said, curiously, when Paul came out.

'Well what?' replied Paul, with infuriating calm.

'What was all that about?' demanded Becky.

'Oh, that! I might tell you later,' said Paul, secretively. So Becky had to be content with that for he set off at a run out of the school gates and along the streets towards home. Becky followed slowly. She was disappointed that Paul had not shared his secret with her. Nor had he said anything about how well she had run that afternoon.

'Are you feeling all right?' asked her mum, when Becky dragged her feet into the kitchen.

'Yes,' answered Becky miserably, dropping her bag on the table.

Paul sauntered in cheerfully.

'Hi, Becky! How's our Olympic champion, then?' he joked.

'Oh, be quiet!' stormed Becky and flew out of the room.

'I think Becky is upset about something,' said Mrs Allen. 'You wouldn't happen to know what it is, would you?'

'Mmmm,' pondered Paul. 'Yes, I think I know what's wrong.' He went to the bottom of the stairs. 'I'm going down to the shed, Becky. See you!' he shouted.

After ten minutes, Becky pushed open the shed door and sat on a box, her back to Paul.

'Look,' said Paul, 'I know why you're sulking.'

'I am not sulking,' snapped Becky.

'You're annoyed because I didn't tell you what I was talking to Miss Shaw about, aren't you?'

Becky spun round. 'Why shouldn't I be? Friends are supposed to share secrets.'

'Because I wanted to wait until we were in the shed. This is a secret no one else must know about, or my life won't be worth living. Now, are you quite ready, or shall I leave it till tomorrow?'

'No, no, go on, tell me!' urged Becky.

Paul settled down on an old stool. 'I stayed behind to tell Miss Shaw that I had chosen a partner for the three-legged race,' he said, carefully.

'I don't see what that has to do with me,' said Becky.

'You will in a minute,' smiled Paul. 'You see, I still have to find out if the person will agree.'

'Oh, I'm sure he will,' enthused Becky. 'You're such a good runner any boy would want to run with you. Is it someone from another class?'

'Er, no,' said Paul. 'Our class!'

'But everyone is paired off except you and me,' puzzled Becky.

'Exactly!' said Paul rocking back, his hands clasped around his knees. Becky looked at him in bewilderment for a moment, then her eyes widened and her hand flew to her mouth.

'Oh, no!' she croaked. 'You don't mean . . .! No you can't . . .! You couldn't . . .!'

'I do!' said Paul cheerfully. 'That's what I stayed behind to talk to Miss Shaw about. She was surprised, but said we could do it if we didn't mind a lot of teasing. Anyway, I asked her if we could keep it a secret until Sports Afternoon. She seemed to think it was a huge joke and said our secret was safe with her.'

Becky was waving her hands about and trying to interrupt. 'Paul, you're absolutely mad! You know how pathetic I am . . .'

'Oh, be quiet!' said Paul firmly. 'You're not pathetic. You weren't this afternoon and you're not going to be pathetic ever again. Now, are you going to run the three-legged race with me, or aren't you?'

Becky sat deep in thought. Then she jumped to her feet.

'All right!' she laughed. 'I'll do it!'

'Great!' said Paul. 'Now, how are we going to practise without anyone seeing us?'

'Well, the garden would do if we asked Mum not to look,' suggested Becky.

So it was that shortly afterwards Mrs Allen found herself working in the kitchen with the blind firmly pulled down to the windowsill. Had she been able to see into the garden, she would have roared with laughter at the sight of Paul and Becky, their legs tied together by a long woolly scarf, trying in vain to struggle from one end of the garden to the other. No matter how they tried, one of them would slither to the ground after two or three steps, pulling the other one over. Usually, it was Becky who hit the ground first.

After a quarter of an hour they gave up in disgust.

'You can come out now!' Becky shouted to her mum, and the blind shot up.

After tea, Paul and Mrs Allen set off once more for the hospital.

'Well, son,' said Mr Walker, 'how's things today?'

'Fine,' said Paul, 'really fine!' His dad looked at him sharply, for he realised that Paul was, in fact, genuinely happy. He reached into his locker and took out some money.

'Here, son! Nip down to the hospital shop and get

yourself some sweets. And before you go, ask Mrs Allen if she'll come over.'

There was a good variety of sweets in the shop and Paul took his time over the selection. He ate a few and tucked the rest into his pocket before wandering back to the ward. Dad and Mrs Allen were deep in conversation, but stopped when they saw him. When visiting time ended, Mrs Allen turned to Paul's dad.

'I'll see about that as soon as I can,' she said.

'Thanks very much,' replied Paul's dad gruffly, and ruffled Paul's hair. Paul was so surprised that he forgot to ask Mrs Allen what she had meant.

Back home Paul shared out the sweets he had bought at the hospital.

'How did you get on there?' mumbled Becky, through a mouthful of marshmallow.

'All right,' said Paul. 'Dad is a lot more cheerful. I just wish . . .'

'What?' asked Becky.

'I wish Mum and Katy would come back,' said Paul, studying a packet of sweets.

'Do you think they will?' asked Becky, not wanting to be too curious.

'I don't know,' replied Paul sadly.

There was nothing Becky could say, so she sat with Paul in silence.

'Come on!' she said suddenly. 'Recorder!'

8

If Paul thought that school was going well, he was about to have his ideas changed. The gang had decided that it was time Paul Walker came down to earth. This friendship with Rebecca Allen would have to stop. That very evening Sandy, Steve, John and Colin were sitting on the swings in the playground plotting Paul's downfall.

'I mean,' said Sandy, 'look at the way he walks to school with that girl – it's appalling!'

'He did say that he had to live at her house,' said Steve, not wanting to be too unfair to his ex-leader.

'That doesn't matter a bit,' answered Sandy, who had taken over as leader. 'He doesn't need to be nice to her at school. I thought we always stuck together, but now he doesn't want anything to do with us.'

This last remark would have amazed Paul. He thought that the gang didn't want to have anything to do with him!

'Well,' said Steve, 'what are you getting at?'

'I think it's time we taught Paul Walker a lesson,' continued Sandy. 'Now, has anybody got any ideas?'

The boys swung idly, each one suggesting dire and dreadful deeds, but they were discarded as being too risky – even downright dangerous. Eventually, they came to a decision. Rather than have one big confrontation, they would annoy Paul in every little way they could. They were full of ideas and shouted them at Sandy.

The list was quite long by the time they had finished and Sandy allocated a couple of tricks to each of them. Well pleased with their evening's work they went home, eagerly awaiting the next day.

On the way to the cloakroom next morning, Paul felt his school-bag being tweaked off his shoulder as Steve ran past.

'Hey! Give me that!' shouted Paul, but it was too late. Steve lobbed the bag on to the flat roof of one of the classrooms and ran into school, laughing.

'Oh, no!' exclaimed Becky. 'What are you going to do?'

'I'll have to find the caretaker and see if he'll bring a ladder,' said Paul, and went off to find Mr Brown.

'If I was you I'd sort out whoever threw your bag up there,' advised Mr Brown, as he carried the ladder through the school. Paul carried one end to please him.

'Right!' agreed Paul, knowing that he couldn't. The caretaker spent a long time positioning his ladder.

'Don't want any accidents, do we?' he said, and slowly climbed on to the roof. It seemed an age before he arrived at the bottom of the ladder with the bag.

'Thanks!' said Paul, and turned to go.

'No more monkey business!' threatened Mr Brown. 'I don't get paid to run after boys' school bags.'

'Where have you been?' asked Miss Shaw, when Paul rushed into the classroom. 'You were nearly marked absent.'

'Sorry, Miss Shaw,' said Paul, 'my bag was lost for a while.'

Miss Shaw wrinkled her brow. 'I don't understand,' she said ominously. Steve held his breath. Would Paul tell tales?

'I had to wait for Mr Brown to get it down from the roof,' said Paul desperately. Miss Shaw looked as if she were going to pursue the matter, then the expression on Paul's face changed her mind.

'Well, sit down and try not to be late again!'

Steve let out a sigh of relief and turned to wink at John who had his fingers crossed under the desk. As Paul walked to his place, he saw a tiny piece of paper on his chair. 'One to us!' it read. Paul swung round to Sandy, but Sandy's head was bent over his maths book. Steve, John and Colin also seemed unsually busy.

With a puzzled shake of the head, Paul shrugged his shoulders and reached into his desk for his maths book. He turned to the page number Miss Shaw had put on the board – at least he tried to. The whole chapter the class had been working through had been stuck together with chewing gum. This was a disaster. Miss Shaw had only last week waged war on the disposal of spent chewing gum. There had been an inspection of the undersides of desks and chairs and Miss Shaw had issued terrible warnings about any further gumming up.

'Why have you not started work yet, Paul Walker?' It was too late! Miss Shaw was already making her way across the classroom. When she saw the maths book, it looked at if words might fail her. Then, unfortunately for Paul, she found her voice and Paul was treated to one of the longest lectures he had ever heard. It was concluded by Miss Shaw ceremoniously dumping Paul's book into the waste bin. 'You will have to share with someone today until I find another book', she said.

Another little slip of paper fluttered on to his desk. 'Two to us!' So that was their game! He turned to glower at the gang members, but they were all working away like beavers. To make matters worse for Paul, it began to rain heavily before lunch, so sports practice was out of the question. By the time four o'clock came, he was more than ready to get out of school. But as he reached for his anorak his hand came in contact with an empty peg.

'I must have put it on the wrong one,' he thought, and wandered along the cloakroom looking at each peg. But his anorak was not there. Becky was ready and walking slowly down to the gate when she heard a shout.

'My anorak's gone!' yelled Paul. 'Go on without me!'

'No fear!' replied Becky. 'You're not safe on your own

today.'

'You again?' barked Mr Brown, as he came to close the cloakrooms. 'What is it this time?'

'I can't find my anorak,' said Paul.

'If you would put things where they are meant to go, you wouldn't cause all this bother,' Mr Brown snapped. 'You'll have to hurry up. I'm locking up in five minutes,' and he went off to check the washbasins. Paul and Becky looked in shoe bags and on windowsills without success.

'Hoy!' came the booming voice of Mr Brown. 'Is this what you're looking for?' He was holding a crumpled blue anorak with white stripes on the sleeves.

'Yes,' shouted Paul, 'that's mine! Where was it?'

'Stuffed down the back of the heating pipes,' said Mr Brown, heavily. 'If you ask me, lad, someone's taking you for a ride. I thought I told you to sort them out.'

'Yes,' said Paul. 'Anyway, thanks for finding it.'

'What's all this about sorting someone out?' asked Becky as they left the building.

'The gang have got it in for me and I can't do a thing about it,' said Paul angrily. He put on his anorak and a piece of paper fell out of the pocket. 'Three to us!' Paul crumpled it up and threw it in a bin.

'You mean the chewing gum as well . . .?' Becky was beginning to put two and two together.

'Yes, that as well! If I get one more lecture today, I think I'll go mad,' and he kicked an empty crisp bag off the pavement.

Becky looked at her watch. 'Help, we're late!' she shouted and they began to run. Mrs Allen was looking at the clock when they burst into the kitchen.

'Where have you been . . .?' she began.

'Please don't say any more, Mum. We're sorry and we've had an awful day at school. If anyone else tells Paul off, he says he's going to go mad!'

'Hmm. Well I can't wait now to hear what has been

going on. Your dad is coming home from work early and I am going out with him for the evening.'

'Where are you going?' asked Becky.

'To see someone,' Mum replied, 'and it's no use asking questions, I haven't got time. I've rung Mrs Jamieson and you're to stay round there till we get back. All right?'

'Oh, yes, that's great!' said Becky. She turned to Paul. 'You'll like Auntie Meg. She's as nutty as a fruitcake!'

'Becky!' said her mother. 'What a dreadful thing to say!'

'I don't mean to be rude, Mum,' said Becky. 'It's just that she does all sorts of odd things. Well, she does, doesn't she?'

'There isn't time to discuss that,' said Mrs Allen, fussing around them. Paul had never seen her in such a rush. The minute Becky's dad arrived home, they all piled into the car.

'Hello, dear!' said Mrs Allen, 'I've brought a picnic tea. If you could drive round by the Jamiesons', we'll drop the children off.'

The car pulled up outside a large house, rather concealed behind enormous bushes in the front garden. There was a brass plate beside the gate: 'Dr P. W. Jamieson'.

'Be good!' called Mrs Allen, as she closed the car door. 'See you later!' And she and Mr Allen drove off down the road.

'I thought I heard a car! Hello, Becky! And you must be Paul!' Paul found himself looking into bright, sparkling eyes not much higher than his own. 'Come into the house!' said Mrs Jamieson, and she led the way along an overgrown path. 'Now, watch your feet!'

Paul and Becky found themselves in a small room outside the back door. Much of the wall space was glass. 'A sort of sun lounge,' said Mrs Jamieson. The floor was covered with bags and from the open ones spilled out what looked like dirty sheep's wool. On the floor was a large expanse of fleece.

'Try not to step on that,' said Mrs Jamieson. 'The farmer only brought it today and I have to sort it and bag it, yet.'

Paul could contain himself no longer. 'Whatever for?' he asked.

'What? Oh, for spinning, dear, spinning!' and Mrs Jamieson pointed to a spinning wheel at the other end of the room.

'Now,' said Mrs Jamieson, as they reached the kitchen without treading on too much wool. 'What would you like? Orange juice, milk, lemonade?'

'Lemonade, please!' chorused two voices.

'Good, good!' said Mrs Jamieson – and then had a problem in finding both the lemonade and the glasses.

'I'm afraid,' she explained, when at last she put their drinks in front of them, 'I'm afraid that when I get a bee in my bonnet about something, I have to keep going at it and everything else gets a bit neglected.' She glanced round the room. 'I'm sure if Peter didn't do the dishes now and then we'd have nothing to eat off. Now, do you mind if I go back to my fleece? It has to be bagged or the oil in it will dry up. Just do whatever you want – I'll be through here if you want me.' She disappeared through the doorway like a small whirlwind, leaving a trail of sheep's wool behind her.

'See what I mean?' said Becky.

'Yes, I do,' agreed Paul. 'Is she always like this?'

'The only time I have seen her sit still for very long is in church. Even then you're not quite sure what she is going to do. I remember one day she dropped the collection plate – that was really funny.'

They finished their drinks and Paul suggested going into the garden. 'It's pretty big, isn't it?' he said.

'Well,' said Becky, 'it's long, but it gets a bit narrow at the bottom. That's a bit of a jungle but there is a path right down.'

'Might be a good place to practise you-know-what,' whispered Paul.

'We haven't got a scarf,' pointed out Becky, 'but I'll ask Auntie Meg.'

They stepped cautiously into the sun lounge. Mrs Jamieson was on her hands and knees, easing apart pieces of fleece.

'Fascinating, this! Absolutely fascinating! Isn't it beautiful?' – and she gave them each a lock of wool. Neither of them could see anything beautiful in the dirty wool.

'Auntie Meg,' said Becky, 'have you an old scarf we could borrow – a long one?'

'Yes, yes! There's an old one of Peter's in the hall cupboard.'

When Becky came back with the scarf, she and Paul went into the garden and tied their legs together – Becky's right to Paul's left.

'One, two, three . . . go!' yelled Paul, and off they went – straight into a rose bush.

'Ouch!' complained Becky, disentangling her hair from the prickles.

'Sorry about that!' said Paul. 'Perhaps we'd better try the other legs.' So they tied Becky's left to Paul's right.

'One, two, three . . . go!' This time they had a little more success, but still only managed a few steps before one of them got out of step and they landed in a heap. When they sat up, they found Mrs Jamieson standing on the path watching them.

'Forgive the interference,' she said, 'but I was a dab hand at the three-legged race when I was at school – or should it be a dab foot?' Seeing their unbelieving faces, she laughed. 'Now, as I recall, the secret is rhythm. You've got to have rhythm. Perhaps a song would help.'

'What do you mean?' asked Becky.

'I think you'll understand better if we try it,' said Auntie Meg. 'Do you know "Old King Cole"? Good!'

In no time at all the bemused children found themselves singing 'Old King Cole' in a very strange way. Every time they put their joined feet down, they sang a word particularly loudly, so it went something like this:

'OLD King COLE was a MERRY old SOUL and a MERRY old SOUL was HE.'

As long as they sang the song, they found that they stayed together. But it was so funny that by the time they reached the end of the garden, they clutched each other, as they fell, laughing, in a heap on the ground.

'That's terrific!' said Paul. 'It really works, Mrs Jamieson!' But Mrs Jamieson was already back in the house.

They practised for a little longer. Each time was better. Each time they sang a bit faster.

'This is a great place to practise,' said Paul. 'Do you think . . .?'

'I was just thinking that myself,' said Becky, and they went to find Mrs Jamieson.

She was sitting at the spinning wheel, pedalling smoothly. They watched the clump of wool change under her fingers into a twisted thread which wound on to the bobbin. All was quiet, except for the whirr of the wheel as it spun round and round. The clump of wool became smaller and smaller until, at last, it had all been spun. Mrs Jamieson wound the end round a knob on the spinning wheel and bent down to an open bag on the floor beside her to take out another handful of wool. Becky took the opportunity to ask her question.

'Auntie Meg! We're practising for the sports and it's all to be a secret, because girls don't usually run with boys. Do you think . . .?'

'Come round here whenever you like,' smiled Mrs Jamieson. 'My lips are sealed.'

'That's funny,' thought Paul. 'We didn't even get round to asking her.'

'My! Is that the time?' said Mrs Jamieson, leaping up from her work. 'Peter will be here in a minute and there isn't a thing ready. Come on!'

She dashed into the kitchen and began pulling open drawers and cupboards.

'Cutlery in there, knives, forks, spoons! Plates in there! We need dinner plates and tea plates. Glasses in there, place mats there!' and she began to wash a lettuce and chop up tomatoes at great speed. Paul and Becky laid the table and generally followed Mrs Jamieson's ever-moving finger. 'Bread in there, butter in the fridge! How are we doing?' They were doing very well, for in next to no time the table was set.

'Hello, dear,' said Mrs Jamieson calmly, as her husband walked in. 'Have you had a busy surgery?'

'Not too bad,' smiled Dr Jamieson, then he noticed Paul and Becky. He grinned at them and turned to his wife. 'You didn't forget the time again, did you?' he asked.

'How did you guess?' said his wife, in mock despair.

'I thought you would be busy with your "fleas". I saw the farmer arrive as I was beginning surgery.'

'Peter,' said Mrs Jamieson, 'you mustn't call it "fleas". The sheep are thoroughly dipped before they are sheared.'

'I know, I know! Only teasing!' Dr Jamieson winked at the children.

'Well, is this food for looking at or eating?' he went on, rubbing his hands together. They all laughed and sat down for their meal. Paul had become quite used to people saying grace before a meal. They had always done so at school, but until he had gone to the Allens' house, he hadn't known that people said it at home, too. Then he heard his name and realised that Dr Jamieson wasn't just asking God to bless the food.

'. . . and, dear Father, we pray for Paul and his father. We also pray for his mum and little Katy. Please show them that you love them.' Then he went on to pray for Mr and Mrs Allen and Becky, before saying 'Amen'.

'Amen!' said Mrs Jamieson, with feeling.

'Now then,' said Mrs Jamieson briskly, 'when we eat in the kitchen, it's S.O.S. – stretch or starve! So you had better get on with it.'

Paul was glad of the activity, as it hid the fact that he was feeling rather strange. That was the first time he had heard anyone talk to God about him – Paul Walker. Yet it had seemed perfectly right and natural.

Becky and Paul couldn't remember ever having had so much fun at a meal before. Dr Jamieson had a fund of funny stories and his wife added extra little details.

After supper, Paul and Becky helped with the dishes, then Mrs Jamieson told them all to stay where they were.

'You've seen a fleece, you've seen me spinning. Now you must see the wonderful bit,' and she darted into the sun lounge.

'Peter, have you seen my niddy-noddy?' she called.

'Her what?' gasped Paul.

'It's in the corner, here,' replied Dr Jamieson, and held up a long piece of wood with cross-pieces at both ends. Around these cross-pieces was wound some spun wool. It was a grey colour with little pieces of grass and grit in it. Paul began to wonder why Mrs Jamieson bothered to do all that work for stuff that looked like dirty string.

Mrs Jamieson carefully took the skein of dirty wool off the niddy-noddy and tied it in several places to stop it tangling up. Then she filled the sink with water and put in some soap powder. 'Watch this!' she said, and took the dirty grey skein and gently swished it around in the bubbles. When she lifted it from the water, Becky gasped with delight, for the wool had become snowy white and softer and fluffier than before.

'That's lovely, Auntie Meg!' she breathed.

'I thought you'd like it,' she said, rinsing the wool in a clean water, 'I always look forward to it myself. It reminds me of that verse in the Bible that says, though our sins are red as crimson they shall be like wool.' And she carefully hung the dripping skein on a wooden rod to dry.

'What are sins?' asked Paul.

'They are the wrong things that we do,' said Dr Jamieson, 'and because God is perfect, they keep us away from him.'

'That's a pity!' said Paul, half to himself.

'But we don't have to stay away, you know,' went on Dr Jamieson. 'God let Jesus, his Son, die for us and take the punishment for the things we do wrong. If we say we are sorry to God and believe that Jesus really died for us, then it is as if the blood of Jesus washes away all our wrong doings, so that God sees us perfect – just like that wool had all the impurities washed away.'

'So you don't do wrong things again?' asked Paul.

'Oh, yes,' laughed Mrs Jamieson. 'We don't want to, but we do. Then we ask God to forgive us and help us to live as he wants us to live.'

Becky had been very quiet, but now she blurted out: 'What do you do when people are being awful to you?' Paul knew that she was thinking of the gang.

'God says we have to love them,' said Dr Jamieson, 'even our enemies. That is really hard. We need God's help to do that.'

There was a question Paul wanted to ask, but he felt he had said enough for one day and was glad when Dr Jamieson pulled out a game of chess and challenged them to beat him. The time flew and although it was quite late when Mr and Mrs Allen arrived to collect Paul and Becky, neither of them felt the least bit tired.

That night, in bed, Paul cast his mind back over the day. What a lot had happened since breakfast! No matter which way he turned he could not get to sleep and he reached for a book from the pile by his bed. Then he remembered the booklet he had brought from Becky's room. He lifted the pile. There it was at the bottom. Would that give him the answer to his question?

He hunched up on his knees, pulling the quilt over his head. 'What is a Christian?' said the cover. Slowly he turned the pages. There were little diagrams with short sentences underneath. It all seemed rather familiar. Then Paul realised that it was just what Dr Jamieson had been talking about. So that was what a Christian was, was it? With a sigh of satisfaction he put down the book and went to sleep.

9

The next morning as Paul left for school, Mrs Allen put a packet of sweets in his pocket.

'For me?' he said, rather surprised.

'Yes! Someone I met last night gave them to me, for you,' said Mrs Allen. 'Now hurry, or you won't get your run before school! And have a good day!' she called after him.

'Not a hope of that!' said Becky, when her mother turned back to the table.

'What do you mean?' asked Mum, sitting down opposite her.

'I can't tell you, Mum, without telling tales, but if all we've got to do is love our enemies, I don't know how we'll get this mess sorted out! Be ready to pick up the pieces when we come home,' said Becky dramatically, and went to pack her school bag.

Meanwhile, Paul was jogging along the pavements, wondering what the gang would have in store for him today. If this vendetta continued, he could see that Miss Shaw would be so cross that she would do something drastic – like banning him from the sports. That would be a catastrophe! What could he do? Should he sort them out as Mr Brown had advised? He could always tell Miss Shaw exactly what was going on, but things would have to be totally desperate before that happened. It was all so unfair. He hadn't even done anything wrong! Then he remembered Dr Jamieson's words. 'God wants us to love people – even our enemies.' Well, Dr Jamieson was a Christian, so that only applied to him, didn't it? Anyway, how would he love the gang, even if he wanted to? The thought of going up to Sandy, Steve, John and Colin and telling them that he loved them was so ludicrous that he laughed out loud. A passing postman gave him a very odd look.

'If that's what you want, God, you'll have to show me how to do it,' he said half aloud – and then shook himself for being so silly.

He met up with Becky and they walked into school together. He kept a tight hold on his schoolbag, but there was no sign of the gang. Instead of leaving his anorak on the peg, he folded it tightly and crammed it into the bottom of his bag. So far, so good! Becky walked beside him all the way to the classroom and Paul sat down with relief. But his relief was short-lived. As Becky looked up, she saw that the board was covered with chalk caricatures of Miss Shaw and Mrs Mitchell. There were silly rhymes as well.

'Look, Paul!' she hissed, and rushed to the board. She was rubbing furiously when a very controlled voice said: 'Put down the board duster!' and she turned to face Miss Shaw.

'Did you draw those, Rebecca Allen?'

'No, Miss Shaw!' said Becky vehemently.

'Very well, we shall wait until everyone else is here before I say any more on the matter.'

The room was ominously quiet as Miss Shaw marked the register. Then she stood up.

'Would the person who did this,' and she waved a hand at the blackboard, 'like to come forward?'

There was dead silence. Each child hoped that the culprit would own up, for Miss Shaw would not let the matter rest. No one walked to the front.

'Very well,' said Miss Shaw, 'we shall carry on with work, but there will be no sports practice today.'

There was a chorus of objections, but Miss Shaw was adamant. There was nothing for it but to do as she said.

A few moments later, as Miss Shaw was moving from one group to another, she stopped and stared very hard at the floor under Paul's desk.

'Paul Walker! Would you kindly bring me that box which is under your desk!' she ordered, chillingly. Silence fell and every eye turned towards Paul. He bent down and his heart sank as he saw an empty box of chalk sticking out of his schoolbag. Slowly, he pulled it out and took it to Miss Shaw.

'Well?' she said. 'What have you to say about this?'

'Nothing, Miss Shaw,' answered Paul, hopelessly, 'I didn't put it there.'

'Have you any idea how it might have got there?' Miss Shaw demanded. Paul had plenty of ideas but he kept them to himself.

'No, Miss Shaw,' he whispered, wishing that the ground would open up and swallow him.

'Then I think that rather clears up the matter of who drew on the blackboard. You will miss sports practice for two days. The rest of the class will have it as usual.'

A muted sigh of relief filled the air and smiles broke out all round the room – except for Becky. She was struggling to hold back the tears. It was so unfair! Paul was being punished and the gang was getting away with it again. She was quite sure by the look on Sandy's face that he and the others had done the drawings and planted the box on Paul. At break she waited behind and cautiously approached Miss Shaw.

'Please, Miss Shaw,' she began, 'Paul Walker didn't do those drawings. They were already there when we came into the classroom.' Miss Shaw looked taken aback.

'I see,' she said, thoughtfully, 'and did you come to school with Paul?'

'Well, not all the way,' said Becky, 'he left before me as he goes for a run first,' and her voice tailed off.

'In which case, he would have had time to come into

school and go out again, wouldn't he?' said Miss Shaw. 'I'm sorry, Becky, but the evidence points to Paul. Now, out you go or you'll miss break.'

Having pulled off such a successful trick, the gang did not bother Paul for the rest of the morning. After lunch, all the others in his class changed their shoes and ran on to the field.

'Come along, Sandy! Why are you so slow?' called Miss Shaw from the door.

'I've left my training shoes at home. I took them to play football last night and forgot to bring them back.'

Miss Shaw tutted impatiently. Games clothes were supposed to be left at school. 'You'd better stay in the classroom as well,' she said.

Over at his desk, something strange was happening to Paul. An odd idea came into his head and almost before he had time to think about it, he heard himself saying: 'Sandy can borrow my trainers, Miss Shaw. We're the same size.' And he handed his shoes to the teacher.

'That's very kind, Paul. Is that all right with you, Sandy?' Sandy's mouth had fallen open in amazement. 'Yes, er, yes!' he gabbled and grabbed the shoes. While he fastened them, his mind was whirling. What was Paul up to? It must be a trick. He ran off after the others, anxious to tell them what had happened. They couldn't make sense of it, either.

As he stared out of the classroom window, Paul was trying to make sense out of it himself. What on earth had he done it for? Then he remembered his bargain with God which he hadn't taken very seriously. Could that be it? He'd have to talk to someone about it.

At four o'clock he and Becky met at the school gate. Paul's anorak was terribly crushed but the sweets in the pocket were intact. They walked to Dr Jamieson's house, sucking as they went.

'Where did you get these?' asked Becky.

'From somebody your mum and dad saw last night,' said Paul.

'I wonder who it was? Funny that they didn't send any for me!'

Paul laughed and took the hint. 'Here, have another few!'

When they walked up the drive of the surgery, they saw several cars parked outside the front door. 'Looks like Dr Jamieson is busy this afternoon,' commented Becky.

They picked their way through the undergrowth at the side of the house and knocked at the door of the sun lounge. Auntie Meg was at her spinning wheel.

'Come on!' she called out. 'The scarf's over there!' Becky and Paul sat down to tie their legs together and then, staggering into the garden, they began to sing:

'OLD King COLE was a MERRY old SOUL . . .' and away they went. It was so exhilarating, Becky thought – almost as if the rhythm of the song was pulling them along. Towards the bottom of the garden they sang faster and faster and landed in the raspberry canes.

'It's really good, isn't it,' gasped Becky. 'I can hardly wait until Sports Afternoon.'

'If I run at all,' said Paul, ruefully. 'The way things are going, I'll probably be banned.'

'That was jolly unfair, today,' said Becky. 'I could thump those boys!'

Paul looked at her in amazement. 'Rebecca Allen, I didn't think you had it in you,' he said, pretending to be shocked. 'Here am I, trying to do it Dr Jamieson's way and you're doing it Mr Brown's way.'

'What do you mean?' asked Becky, as she untied the scarf.

So Paul explained what had happened about the training shoes. 'I don't quite understand it,' he said at last.

'Let's go and ask Auntie Meg what she thinks,' suggested Becky. 'She won't tell anyone else.'

'Finished already?' smiled Auntie Meg, as they stood beside her.

'We want to ask you something,' said Becky.

'Ask away,' said Auntie Meg, her hands working the fleece on her apron.

When Paul had told the tale of the day's events, she stopped spinning and looked at him.

'It seems to me, Paul, that you have learned a very important lesson. God tells us that we ought to repay evil with good. It is one of the hardest things he asks us to do. Had you kept your trainers to yourself, you would certainly have had your revenge in a small way. But you repaid evil with good.' Auntie Meg took off her apron. 'Very interesting! Now, I expect you wouldn't say no to a glass of lemonade.'

When they had finished their drinks, Becky stood up to leave. 'We oughtn't to be too late for tea, it's hospital tonight, isn't it?' Paul nodded in agreement.

'In that case, I'll run you home in Rattlecrash,' said Auntie Meg.

'Wait till you see this,' whispered Becky, as they followed Auntie Meg round to the front of the house. Auntie Meg was opening the doors of one of the most decrepit cars Paul had ever seen. When she saw his hesitation, she assured him that Rattlecrash would get him home.

'A wheel did come off once, I remember, but I wasn't going fast at the time.' Not much comforted, Paul climbed into the back seat beside Becky. At the third attempt, the engine sprang to life and they jolted on to the road.

'I'm afraid she's a bit like me,' explained Auntie Meg, over her shoulder – 'a bit slow when she's woken up!' Paul noticed an earwig behind the glass of the speedometer and pointed it out to Becky. 'It's been there as long as I can remember,' she whispered.

Despite one or two ominous crunches from the gear

box, they reached home safely.

'Thanks, Auntie Meg!' said Becky.

'No trouble!' shouted Auntie Meg, above the noise of the engine. 'See you tomorrow!' and with a grinding of gears, she drove off.

As they watched her go, Becky said emphatically: 'Everybody should have an Auntie Meg!' Paul couldn't help but agree.

Mr Walker was much more cheerful that evening when Paul went to visit him. 'This'll be the last time you need come,' he said. 'I'm coming home on Saturday.'

'What about Friday night?' asked Paul.

'Oh, er, no need to come then,' said Dad, awkwardly.

'We may be busy at your house on Friday night,' put in Mrs Allen. 'We'll need to have everything ready for Saturday.'

As it was Paul's last visit, Dad gave him some money to spend at the hospital shop and off he went. When he returned later on, his dad and Mrs Allen were still chatting.

'That's settled, then,' his dad was saying.

'What is?' asked Paul.

'Nothing to bother you,' said his dad. 'Now come and help me finish this jigsaw. That occupational therapy woman gave it to the chap in the next bed and he went home today.'

At the end of visiting time, Paul looked round the ward. He had become used to the hospital, but he would be glad to have Dad back home. In the car he asked Mrs Allen what there was to get ready at his house.

'There's plenty to do,' she said. 'We'll need to let in some fresh air and we could clean the windows while we are at it. Then there'll be the beds to change, the fridge to defrost . . .' Paul stopped listening. It was obvious that Mrs Allen was not going to be satisfied with anything less than a spring clean.

'Thank goodness I'm at school,' he thought.

'So you and Becky,' continued Mrs Allen, 'will be able to come round and help after you have been at Auntie Meg's – though why you should have to go there every day, I don't know.'

Becky was waiting for them and she and Paul disappeared down to the shed.

'You haven't forgotten about the recorder, have you?' asked Becky and stood over him while he did his practice. The thought occurred to Paul that Becky was very like her mother! When he had played to her satisfaction, he put the recorder down.

'What are we going to do about the gang tomorrow?' he asked. 'After this afternoon I don't know what to do next.'

'I think you'd better do what you did today,' said Becky, thoughtfully.

'What? Lend Sandy my trainers again? He'll have his own,' said Paul.

'No, I didn't meant that! You told Auntie Meg that you had asked God to show you what to do.'

'I didn't exactly ask,' said Paul. 'It was more of a bargain.'

'Well, whatever it was, why not do it again tomorrow?'

'I'm not sure,' said Paul. He wondered if he was expecting rather too much of God. Suddenly, he leapt out of the shed and ran to the back door. Becky was surprised by his quick exit. 'I didn't think we had finished,' she said to herself as she followed him into the house. Paul was having a drink and seemed keen to go to bed. He crammed a couple of biscuits into his mouth, said a rather muffled 'Goodnight' and went upstairs. Mrs Allen looked at the clock and then at Becky.

'Have you had another argument?' she enquired. 'It's not like Paul to go to bed so early.'

'No, we haven't, said Becky. 'I don't know what's wrong with him,' and she trailed through to the lounge to do her piano practice.

Upstairs, Paul had changed into his pyjamas, but was not thinking of sleep. He had things on his mind that needed to be sorted out. There were Dad and Mum and the row they had had. And these people, Mr and Mrs Allen, who were like his dad and mum in lots of ways, yet very different in others. There were Auntie Meg and Dr Jamieson. They were different, too – what was it? The only thing he could think of was that the Allens and Jamiesons talked about God as if he really was their father – and a good one, at that. 'It must be great to have someone like that around. God doesn't go away and leave you or end up in hospital,' argued Paul to himself. Then there was the business of wrong things being forgiven and forgotten, that Dr Jamieson had told him about.

What was it Dr Jamieson had said? 'If we are sorry and believe that Jesus died for us . . .' Paul screwed his eyes up tight. Then he opened them and looked out of the window at the sky.

'Hello, God,' he said, hesitantly. 'I hope you're listening, because this is me, Paul Walker. I've done lots of wrong things and I'm sorry about them. Thank you very much for letting Jesus die for me. I'd like you to be my father, too – if that's all right with you, er, Amen. Oh, and would you please show me what to do about the gang.'

Paul lay down on his bed. 'I'm glad that's sorted out,' he murmured, and smiled as he settled down to sleep.

10

Mrs Allen stood at the kitchen door next morning, armed with buckets, rubber gloves and all manner of cleaning things.

'Come on, you two!' she said, fussing round them like a sheepdog. 'I've got work to do today.'

'Dad doesn't come home for two days yet,' said Paul.

'It takes a day or two to wash and dry sheets, you know. I might just do a pair of curtains . . . Now I expect to see you at Paul's house no later than five o'clock,' and she bustled them out of the house.

'I didn't think our house was all that dirty,' Paul said to Becky, thoughtfully.

'It wouldn't need to be,' explained Becky. 'Sometimes Mum calls it "freshening the place up" and there's no answer to that.'

They were overtaken by Becky's mum clutching dusters and buckets, the keys to Paul's house jingling in her pocket. 'Have a good day!' she called as she disappeared up the path of Paul's house.

'Poor house!' giggled Becky. 'You won't know what has hit you by tonight.'

'Come on!' said Paul. 'Race you to the corner! I haven't had my run today! Let's go the long way round, we've got time,' and he jogged slowly so that Becky could keep up with him. In the distance they could see a group of boys in the park.

'Hey, look! There's Steve and John,' panted Becky. 'What's going on?'

Steve and John were sitting on the swings and it

appeared that two older boys were telling them to get off. When Steve and John refused, the bigger boys ripped open their school-bags and threw their books high in the air. One landed on top of the swing frame, another fell into the litter bin and the rest scattered on the ground. Steve and John leapt off the swings, arms flailing and flew at the two older boys.

'The idiots!' said Paul. 'They don't stand a chance with those two bullies.'

Becky looked at Paul. 'Should we do anything?' she asked warily. Paul hesitated but only for a split second.

'Where's the whistle?' he said. 'It's worth a try.'

He grabbed the whistle from Becky and ducked behind a garden wall. This time Paul gave three loud blasts. The bigger boys paused in the fight to look round to see where the noise was coming from. Steve and John seized the opportunity to wriggle free and run for it. It was nearly nine o'clock and the older boys obviously decided that a chase wasn't worth the trouble. They wandered off in the direction of the senior school. Paul and Becky eased out from behind the wall.

'We'd better hurry,' said Paul, 'we're going to be late.'

'What about their books?' said Becky, anxiously. Paul was already jogging off to school. 'Leave them!' he called.

'It's no good, I can't,' muttered Becky to herself and ran across to where the two bags lay. She began stuffing the books into them and was just wondering how she would get the one down from the frame, when Paul said: 'OK You hold the seat steady while I climb up the chain.' He retrieved the book and it was put safely into one of the bags. The school bell rang in the distance.

'Run!' shouted Paul, but they were a good five minutes late getting into the classroom. Miss Shaw looked point-edly at them as they panted in. She watched as they walked to her table, each of them dropping a bag on the way. She also noticed the looks of astonishment which passed between Steve and John.

'Rebecca Allen, it's not like you to be late. What is your excuse?'

'I'm very sorry, Miss Shaw,' said Becky, 'I was delayed.'

'Delayed? Hmmm.' Miss Shaw did not appear to be satisfied with that answer. 'I expect you were "delayed" too,' she said, turning to Paul.

'Yes, Miss Shaw,' said Paul.

'Then I'm afraid I shall have to "delay" you in class-room at break. Go and sit down.'

Paul and Becky went to their seats and exchanged sympathetic glances. Meanwhile, John and Steve were sorting out their school-bags, discovering with relief that nothing was missing.

'I don't get it,' whispered John, 'fancy making them-selves late for us!'

Sandy turned round. 'What's going on?' he hissed.

'Tell you later,' said John in a hoarse whisper as Miss Shaw walked in their direction.

Paul's group was painting that morning and his mind was free to think over what had happened. Again, he had helped the gang in a way he could never have imagined. And he realised that there had been a choice – whether or not to help. Perhaps that kind of choice had always been there but he had never noticed. He had always chosen the way which would suit him best.

'Always look after number one,' Dad had said. Paul wasn't so sure now.

'Thanks, God!' he said under his breath.

At break time, he and Becky stayed in their seats while the rest of the class clattered out into the sunshine.

'What am I going to do with you two?' sighed Miss Shaw. 'Is there anything wrong that I ought to know about? You were getting on so nicely, Paul.' She was so genuinely perplexed that Becky was tempted to tell the whole story, but she checked herself just in time.

'Are you still running together in the three-legged race?' asked Miss Shaw, realising that neither of them was prepared to talk.

'Oh, yes!' they said together with such enthusiasm that Miss Shaw almost regretted her doubts about their behaviour. She smiled: 'Your secret is still safe, but please, no more trouble. Now off you go, your five minutes is up!'

'She's not so bad, is she?' said Paul when they were outside.

'I don't know. You're used to being ticked off,' replied Becky.

They turned the corner on to the field and two boys stepped in front of them blocking their way. There was complete silence for what seemed a long time as the two pairs of children stared at each other. Then Steve cleared his throat.

'Look!' he said, slowly, 'thanks for getting our books for us.'

'Er, yes – thanks!' agreed John.

Again there was a pause before Paul said casually: 'That's all right. Fancy a sweet?' With that, the four of them squatted on the grass to share what was left of the bag of sweets.

Sandy Graham watched from a distance. 'So much for loyalty!' he thought.

'Why not forget it?' said Colin, his one remaining ally. 'I can't even remember what we're fighting about,' and he sidled across to the group on the grass before the sweets ran out. Sandy kicked a stone. It was no fun being alone. Then he noticed that Paul had stood up and was walking towards him. He braced himself for a fight.

'There's one left,' said Paul, holding out the almost empty bag to Sandy. Sandy gave a rueful grin. 'Hope it hasn't got nuts in,' he said, fishing the sweet out.

The next evening, Paul had to admit that Mrs Allen's hard work had been worth it. His house smelled fresh and clean, everywhere was tidy. There was even a vase of flowers in the lounge.

'Now, I want to show you where I have put things,' Mrs Allen said to Paul. She led him from the fridge to the cupboards and explained what was in them. Paul was taken aback at the number of boxes and tins in the cupboards. No wonder she and Dad had talked a lot! Then they locked the back door and walked the few yards to Becky's house.

'This will be your last night here,' said Becky sadly, as they sat in the kitchen watching Mrs Allen getting the tea ready.

'I suppose it is,' said Paul.

'Now there's no need to be miserable about it,' broke in Mrs Allen. You live very near each other and Paul will be welcome here whenever he feels like coming.'

'It won't be the same,' moaned Becky.

'No, it won't,' agreed her mum, 'but you'll get used to it.' Becky doubted that, but said no more.

'As the house is ready,' said Paul, changing the subject, 'should I go to see Dad this evening?'

'No!' said Mrs Allen sharply. Then seeing Paul's surprised look, she added: 'Your dad isn't expecting you and anyway, I believe he may be having another visitor tonight.'

Paul wondered who that could be but Mrs Allen left the room abruptly to call her husband in from the garden for his tea.

It was a good tea. There were muffins with strawberry jam, a chocolate cake with cream inside and sweets on top, plates of crisps and a bowl of fruit. After licking the last bit of cream off his fingers, Paul leant back in his chair. 'That was terrific,' he said. 'Thanks a lot!' And then he added: 'And thanks a lot for having me stay here.' Then, overcome by embarrassment, he tickled Ruff under the chin.

'We've enjoyed having you,' said Mrs Allen. 'Now if you two have finished, you can disappear while I clear away.'

'And I'll help.' said Mr Allen, putting his arm round his wife.

Down at the shed, Becky and Paul felt rather too full to do anything much. 'I'm not sure that I could blow into the recorder,' said Paul feebly.

'None of that! I know your tricks,' laughed Becky. 'Get on with it!'

After his practice, Paul put down the recorder and sat deep in thought.

'You know,' he said eventually, 'I feel really odd. Half of me is pleased that Dad is coming out of hospital and I'll be back with him. The other half doesn't want to go back home at all.'

'That's because you'll miss me,' said Becky confidently.

'I don't think so,' said Paul slowly. 'I think it's because my house won't be like home without Mum and Katy.'

Becky looked out of the window. She didn't know what to say to Paul – home without Mum would be strange. They sat, busy with their thoughts until Ruff pushed his way through the half-open door and ran from one to the other, hitting their legs with his tail. Then he sat in the middle of the floor, his head on one side, looking at them hopefully.

'Want a walk?' asked Paul. At the word 'walk', Ruff went into his acrobatic routine, leaping round them and barking furiously.

'All right, all right!' laughed Becky, trying to avoid Ruff's sharp claws, 'We'll take you out.'

As they passed Paul's house, Ruff racing beside them, Becky said: 'Will you still be able to come to Auntie Meg's on Monday and Tuesday?'

'I hope so,' said Paul. 'It's not long until Wednesday

and we need all the practice we can get.'

At bedtime, neither of them wanted to go to bed and they dawdled about the kitchen having extra drinks, or giving Ruff one final stroke before he jumped into his basket for the night. When they did go upstairs, however, they were soon asleep and it seemed hardly a minute before it was Saturday morning and Mrs Allen was calling them down to breakfast.

'How is Dad coming home?' asked Paul.

'I'll go and fetch him after I drop Becky off. She can always stay at the music teacher's house if I take too long,' explained Mr Allen.

After breakfast, Paul helped Mrs Allen to carry some milk along to his own house.

'You're very quiet, Paul,' said Mrs Allen, as she put the milk in the fridge. 'I'll switch the kettle on and we'll have a cup of tea ready for your dad.'

Paul sat at his own kitchen table and Mrs Allen came to sit beside him. 'Do you still think my mum loves me?' Paul asked quietly, his eyes on the table.

'I'm sure she does, Paul,' replied Mrs Allen, taking one of his hands in her own. Paul looked up into her face and smiled.

'Right!' he said, with a sigh of relief.

The cups were on the table beside the teapot when Dad arrived. He walked through the back door and looked round the kitchen.

'My, but it's good to be home!' he said. 'I'd almost forgotten what it looked like – and a fresh cup of tea!' he dropped his case on the floor and sat down. Mr Allen was standing at the door.

'We'll be off then,' he said.

'Let me know if you need anything,' said Mrs Allen. 'Paul knows where most things are. Cheerio!' And with that, she and Mr Allen were gone.

'Lost your tongue?' asked Dad, not unkindly.

'Oh, no, Dad!' Paul came back to life. 'I'm glad you're home,' but his smile quickly faded.

Mr Walker noticed it but said nothing. He had had a strange time in hospital and had made discoveries of his own about people who cared. He had also realised things about himself – and some of them none too pleasant.

For the rest of the morning, he and Paul wandered about the house, putting clothes away and looking in cupboards.

'Where did all this stuff come from?' asked Dad, opening a tin of cakes and another of biscuits.

'I thought you asked Mrs Allen to get it for you,' said Paul.

'Not me!' said Dad. 'There's enough here to feed an army!'

'I think there are two salads in the fridge for our dinner,' said Paul.

'That's good! I was wondering how I could face going to the chip shop,' laughed Dad.

The day dragged on. Time had slowed down and Paul lay in front of the television most of the afternoon and early evening.

'Look, son!' said Dad. 'There's no point staying in with me. Why not go out to play? I don't mind.'

'Can I?' said Paul, leaping to his feet. 'You'll be all right?'

' 'Course I will – I'm not an invalid!'

Paul didn't need a second telling. He was down the road in two minutes and outside Becky's kitchen door. Perhaps he ought to knock, now that he didn't live there.

'I thought we'd got rid of you,' joked Mr Allen from the back garden. 'Go in, they'll be pleased to see you!'

Paul pushed open the door and Ruff set up such a barking that Becky and her mum rushed through to see what was the matter.

'Come in, come in!' said Mrs Allen, laughing. Becky

stood with a huge grin on her face.

'I can't stay long,' said Paul, 'but Dad said I could go out and play.'

'You'd better do that, then,' smiled Mrs Allen.

An hour later, Paul returned to his house feeling much better. He now knew that he could still feel welcome in the Allens' house and he whistled quietly to himself as he made a cup of tea for his dad.

'You've perked up a bit,' said Dad, as he drank his tea. 'Who were you playing with?'

'Um, Becky Allen,' said Paul, with a wry smile.

'It's "Becky" now, is it?' said Dad. 'What happened to "R.A."? Never mind, son, I'm only joking. We can all change our minds about people.'

Paul was curious to know what he meant. However, Mr Walker didn't want to talk any more and put the cups in the sink.

'We'll do those in the morning,' he said, 'it's an early night for us.'

He locked the doors and went up to bed. Paul followed reluctantly.

Next morning Paul woke with a start. He couldn't think where he was or what day it was. When he remembered, he looked at the clock. It was half past nine already. The Allens would be getting ready for church. A few minutes later he heard their car start up and looked out of the window in time to see it go past. In his mind's eye he imagined Becky sitting in church with her dad and mum. He wondered whether anybody would notice that he wasn't with them. Perhaps one day Dad would let him go to church. There was so much he wanted to find out about God and it seemed a good place to start.

11

It was a relief when Monday morning came, but Paul was mildly surprised to find Dad up and shaved by eight o'clock.

'What are you up so early for?' asked Paul. 'You're not at work this week.'

'I'm going out for the day,' replied Dad, guardedly. 'I'll be back at tea-time.'

'Where are you going?' enquired Paul.

'Oh, around and about,' said Dad, and Paul knew he would get no more explanation than that. He set off on his run, making sure he was in time to meet Becky at the usual place. She greeted him like a long lost friend.

'Only two more days to go,' said Paul, as they made their way to the gate. They were hailed by Sandy and Colin.

'By the way, Paul,' said Sandy, 'about the three-legged race . . .'

'Don't worry about that,' interrupted Paul, 'it's all under control,' and he ran into the cloakroom.

'Whatever did he mean by that?' asked a mystified Sandy.

That afternoon, Paul and Becky worked hard at Auntie Meg's. Suddenly Becky stopped, and said, 'I wonder what the boys will say on Wednesday?'

'I'm not sure,' said Paul. 'They seem quite happy about me being friends with you now. It's the first time we've ever settled a gang dispute without a fight.'

'But they didn't ever say sorry for the rotten tricks, did they? And they didn't get into trouble with Miss Shaw, like you did. Don't you think they ought to?'

Paul had to admit that he had felt it was a bit unfair. The gang had not paid for what they had done, particularly the blackboard incident. 'On the other hand,' he said, 'they did have to change their minds about me. I expect that was hard.'

Auntie Meg was interested to know how Paul's dad was, and gave Paul a cake tin to take home.

Paul's dad was home before him and had made the tea. 'Another cake?' he said, as Paul put the tin on the table. 'Who sent this one?'

'Auntie Meg . . . I mean, Mrs Jamieson.'

'Not Dr Jamieson's wife?' asked Dad.

'Mmmm,' said Paul, his mouth full of cake.

'How did you meet her?'

Paul explained about Mrs Jamieson looking after him while Mr and Mrs Allen had gone to visit someone. 'I don't know who it was, but I don't think they lived very near. Mr Allen had to come home from work early.' Dad did not appear to be interested in that and continued asking Paul about Dr and Mrs Jamieson.

'So why were you round there tonight?'

Paul racked his brain for an answer. 'Er, well, I had to collect this cake.' It was the truth – if not the whole truth.

'By the way,' said Dad, 'I have had a letter from the athletics club. They say you can join for one session a week on a Friday evening. Do you want to?'

'Wow!' said Paul. 'Do I want to!'

'It costs a bit,' said Dad, 'but I think you could do with a treat. I'll run you there in the car.'

Paul could hardly believe his ears. An athletics club! When Dad was settled in front of the television, Paul asked if he could go out.

'Sure, son! Don't be late!'

Paul raced down to Becky's house and ran into the kitchen. Mr Allen was mending a washer on the tap.

'I'm going to the athletics club! I'm going to the athletics club!' Paul shouted, jumping up and down with excitement. Mr Allen looked up with a grin on his face.

'Oh, that's good, Paul! Really good! I'm so pleased. Go through and tell Becky.' Becky was delighted with the news.

'Will you tell me everything they teach you?' she asked.

'I'll think about it,' he said, 'but I must be off now. What with the club and sports the day after tomorrow, I don't think I'll sleep tonight.'

Tuesday arrived and with it a flurry of activity. Mrs Mitchell called the whole school on to the field to show them where to sit until it was their turn to run. She liked these occasions to go without a hitch. Then she read out the order in which the races would be run. Paul and Becky did not know whether to be relieved or disappointed when they heard that the three-legged race would be the final event of the afternoon.

'At least we'll avoid being teased by everyone,' said Paul. 'They'll be too keen to get home.'

When Mrs Mitchell had sorted out every last detail she gave them a short lecture.

'The main thing is to enjoy yourselves,' she said. 'Try as hard as you can but remember, not everyone can win. Do your best and I, for one, will be pleased.'

Becky wasn't sure that she would enjoy herself, but she was certainly going to try very hard. Mum would be there and Becky desperately wanted to show her how she had improved. Paul, too, was keen to do well in front of his dad.

'You will be there tomorrow afternoon?' he asked Dad that evening.

'Where?' asked Dad, putting down his paper.

'Oh, Dad, you can't have forgotten! The school sports!'

'Ah, yes, the sports! Mmmm! I'll be there.'

'You won't forget, Dad? Two o'clock on the school

field!'

'Yes, yes, I said I'd be there, didn't I?' said Dad impatiently.

Paul did not press the matter further. He went to bed early and lay for a long time, thinking about the next day. He had looked forward to it for so long and now it was almost upon him! He hoped that Dad would be proud of him.

Wednesday dawned as clear and sunny as Paul could have wished for. He couldn't stay in bed and was out running on the pavements before eight o'clock. After breakfast he checked once more that Dad was sure of the time to be at school and then ran to Becky's house.

'How do you feel?' he asked Becky, when she opened the door.

'Sick!' she replied. Paul had to agree that she did look a bit pale.

'Really sick?' he asked, seeing the three-legged race disappear before his very eyes.

'No, no!' said Mrs Allen. 'Becky's always like this when she's nervous – though what there is to be nervous about, I don't know.' She turned to Becky: 'After all, you are only doing what all the other girls are doing, aren't you?'

That's what you think! thought Becky. Just wait till this afternoon! But out loud she said: 'I'll be all right once I get to school,' and she grabbed her bag and kissed Mum. 'See you this afternoon!'

'I'll be there,' said Mum, 'don't worry!'

Paul decided that a jog might help to calm Becky's nerves.

'What are you bothered about, anyway?' he asked.

Becky bit her lip before replying. 'It's the three-legged race.'

'What about it?' enquired Paul.

'It's just that . . . well . . . you said that you wanted to win all the races. What if you don't? I mean, it'll be my fault . . .' and she stopped running. Paul came to a standstill.

'D'you know,' he said, 'it doesn't seem so important now, to win all the races.' He was surprised to hear himself say that, but it was true.

'Tell you what, R.A. If we make it to third place, I'll never call you R.A. again.'

Becky laughed and pushed him into a hedge. 'You haven't called me R.A. for ages, anyway. So that's no great reward!' But she was relieved to know that Paul wouldn't be broken-hearted if they didn't win the race.

By a quarter to two, all the classes were sitting on the ground along one side of the track, while parents started arriving in ones and twos and were shown to the rows of chairs on the other side. Becky kept her eyes on the gate and felt a rush of excitement when she saw her mum arrive. She was surprised to see that Mr Walker was with her.

'Look who's here!' she whispered to Paul, who was sitting in the row behind her.

'Oh, good, he remembered!' said Paul. All morning he had doubted whether his dad would be there. Now he had even more reason to do well.

Shortly after two o'clock, Mrs Mitchell walked to the prize table and tapped the microphone to check it was switched on.

'Good afternoon, everyone!' she said. 'Welcome to our annual sports!' Then she made a speech about the value of such events. Just when Paul thought she was never going to stop, she announced the first race and sat down.

Paul waited impatiently, tapping his finger on his knees. Eventually, it was the turn of their class. Miss Shaw lined them up and they walked down to the start. The girls raced first. Becky put all she had into her running and scraped in fifth. Paul saw Mrs Allen clapping vigorously. Then it was Paul's turn. He lined up with the five other boys and waited, tense as a bow. When the whistle blew, he was off like an arrow, his head thrown back and his arms beating the air. Half-way along the track he heard another boy close behind, threatening his position. Paul forged ahead and the winning tape dropped as he burst through it, a clear first! He bent over to recover his breath and then looked along the row of parents. Dad and Mrs Allen were smiling and applauding enthusiastically.

The other classes all ran a race before it was Miss Shaw's class again. Once more they walked to the start, whilst another teacher laid the hurdles across the track for the next race. Paul was pleased to see that this time Becky came fourth. One or two of the girls had tripped over the hurdles, but Becky cleared every one. The look on her face as she crossed the line made all Paul's coaching worthwhile. She had not disgraced herself this year!

When his turn came, Paul found himself standing between Sandy and John. 'Now I'll show them!' he said to himself, and crouched down for the start. He got away well, but Sandy had been practising too and was at his shoulder.

'Come on, Paul!' came a shout. It was Dad. 'Right!' thought Paul. He streaked away from Sandy, hardly noticing the last few hurdles, so firmly was his eye fixed on the tape. The race was his! For the second time he collected his prize ticket from Mrs Mitchell. Dad was on his feet, clapping loudly and proudly informing those around him that Paul was his son.

'Two down,' mused Paul, 'and one to go!'

Once the hurdles had been cleared away, each class ran a different race. A sack race was followed by the egg and spoon and then the obstacle race. While this was underway, Miss Shaw once again led her class to the start. She handed out scarves to them and pairs of boys and girls began tying their legs together. Miss Shaw looked quizzically at Paul and Becky, but they shook their heads. They were going to leave it to the very last minute!

The first group from their class set off along the track amid chuckles from the parents as, one after another, the couples fell over. It was even funnier to watch them struggling to their feet. Meanwhile the second group of couples were so engrossed in the race that they did not notice Paul and Becky quickly tie their legs together. The first race ended with a couple of girls first, followed closely by two boys. The remaining couples lined up at the start and only then did they notice the extra couple at the end. A ripple of amazement passed along the line and Paul and Becky found themselves the object of disbelieving stares. Paul and Becky were concentrating too hard to notice much. As Miss Shaw said, 'Ready, steady!' they were singing under their breath, 'OLD King COLE was a . . .'

The whistle blew and they were off! Paul and Becky sang quietly as they thumped their legs down together '. . . and a MERRY old SOUL was HE. . .' They were doing well – only two couples remained ahead of them. But Becky was so intent on getting the rhythm right that she forgot to sing under her breath!

'OLD King COLE was a MERRY old SOUL . . .' rang out across the field. The spectators began to laugh and Paul screwed up his face in disgust. But the track was longer than Auntie Meg's garden and Becky hadn't enough breath to keep singing. She and Paul began to run raggedly and were in danger of falling.

'Ah well,' thought Paul. 'There's nothing else for it, I suppose,' and he took up the tune, singing as loudly as he could, '. . . and a MERRY old SOUL was HE.'

Surprise, as well as the rhythm, gave Becky new energy and they managed to overtake one couple. They thumped on towards the line with great determination, and fell across it – inches behind the winners.

They lay still for a moment, gasping for breath. Then Paul untied the scarf and heaved Becky to her feet. They walked over to the table to collect their prize ticket. Mrs Mitchell was dabbing her eyes with a handkerchief and had difficulty in speaking.

'Well done!' she said. 'Well done, a fine race!' and she appeared to be overtaken by a fit of coughing.

As that had been the last event, parents and children were beginning to stream off the field. Paul wondered what his dad had thought of his running and turned to find him. He saw Mrs Allen, but his dad was not with her. He was standing a little distance away, next to another woman. A woman with a child in a pushchair! A woman he recognised!

'Mum!' he shrieked across the field, 'Mum!' Regardless of anyone, he ran faster than he had run all afternoon and flung his arms round her waist. Her hand stroked his hair, and she hugged him close.

'Hello, Paul,' said his mum, very quietly. 'Come on, let's all go home.'

Much later that evening, Paul and Becky sat in the shed. 'I can't stay long,' said Paul. 'But I had to come and explain it all. You see, your mum and dad had a lot to do with it.'

'With what?' asked Becky.

'With my mum coming home,' smiled Paul. 'You see, your mum spoke to mine on the phone, only she couldn't tell me. My mum thought it would upset me.'

Becky was becoming confused.

'D'you remember the evening we were left at the Jamiesons'?' asked Paul. Becky nodded. 'Well, your dad and mum had gone to see my mum. Dad asked them to go. Then Mum visited him in hospital – that was why I couldn't go last Friday. Then Dad went to see Mum on Monday and she decided to come home.' And Paul grinned with satisfaction. 'Anyway, I'll have to go now.

Oh, by the way . . .'

'Yes?' said Becky.

'Thanks for the three-legged race – it was the best of the lot!'

With that, Paul was away running to his house. He let himself in quietly so that he wouldn't disturb Dad and Mum. They had been in the lounge for an hour or more, sitting beside each other on the sofa, talking.

'We're going to give it another try,' Dad had said earlier, 'but we've a lot to straighten out.'

Paul tiptoed upstairs and peeped into Katy's room. She lay sound asleep, one arm thrown above her head, the other across her teddy. Under the cot were two small red slippers. Paul gazed at her for several minutes, hardly believing that she was really there, before going to his own room.

When his mum came to say goodnight, he put his arms around her neck. There were so many things he wanted to tell her – so many discoveries about loving and being loved. He wanted to tell her about his special friend so that she need never feel lonely again. But it could wait. There would be plenty of time.

'Goodnight, Paul,' said Mum, switching off the light.

'Goodnight, Mum.'

If you have enjoyed this book you may like to know about these other recent **Leopard Books**.

The Eye of Time and Space
Dorothy Webb
Christine meets a mysterious stranger who gives her a box through which she can travel into the past.

The box brings many exciting discoveries which have unexpected effects on Christine and the others in her class.

Code Red on Starship Englisia
Mark A. Durstewitz
During a space flight, Howard has to go outside the ship to repair it. He almost loses his life, but is saved by a strange light. His efforts to discover who or what it was lead to sinister attacks on the faith he was beginning to discover.

To Catch a Golden Ring
Marilyn Cram Donahue
Angie longs to get away from the shabby street where her family lives. She and Con plan a dream future but then disaster strikes. Angie has to grapple with some tough questions. An exciting and moving story.